I0679011

Ghoulies and Ghosties and Long-leggedy Beasties

And Things that go Bump in the Night

Jannette Quackenbush

Copyright © 2025 by Jannette Quackenbush

ISBN-13: 978-1-940087-70-2

"From ghoulies and ghosties and long-leggedy beasties and things that go bump in the night, Good Lord deliver us." An old prayer by an unknown author

Alabama
Huggin' Molly

Nestled in the heart of southeastern Alabama is the quaint town of Abbeville, known for its tree-lined streets and retro feel. However, beneath its charming exterior lurks a gaunt, ghoulish woman dressed in black, hiding in the shadows as dusk falls, waiting for the lonely to pass by. She wears a black hat that casts ominous shadows over her face and is cloaked in a veil that obscures her features in darkness.

As she prowls the desolate streets, a sense of dread hangs in the air—she waits for a solitary walker to catch her eye. In that instant, a primal fear grips her prey, consuming them entirely.

They instinctively try to escape. With a chilling hunger, she springs into action, her long, gaunt legs prancing in high-kneed kicks, her movements silent and swift. As she closes the distance, skinny, too-long arms stretch out, and her skeletal embrace becomes a suffocating, terrifying grip. Her eerily cold, long fingers are constrictive, wrapping around her victims with an unnatural strength. In that heart-stopping moment, the hug shifts from a false sense of safety to a deadly conclusion, leaving only whispers of her existence behind in the night. Only then does she emit her dreadful, blood-curdling scream.

She is called Huggin' Molly. In the late 1800s and mid-1900s, she prowled nightly for lonely pedestrians, especially little children, from the shadows. When she spotted a victim, she would leap out and chase them with incredible speed and great stealth. The community learned to avoid the cemetery and the local Baptist Church at night, as these were the familiar haunts of Huggin' Molly.

In the late 1930s, a young man named Bun Gamble walked home along Trawick Street after a late movie, blissfully unaware that he was being followed. Just as he was about to reach his house, a tall figure draped in dark clothing emerged from a ditch beside the road, blocking his path. Huggin' Molly! His heart raced. Fortunately, Bun had enough distance between himself and the ghoul—he turned and escaped into the light of town just as her skeletal fingers snapped just inches behind him, catching only air. He felt the rush of wind from her fingers graze his neck.

In the 1940s, Donald Clenney owned a home on Elm Street, a time before sidewalks were added and when the roadway was unlit by streetlights. This tree-lined section of town was pitch black at night. One evening, Clenney heard a loud "wham" against the outside wall of his house.

Cautiously, he stepped out onto the porch and discovered a young man lying unconscious in the grass beside his home. Clenney quickly knelt beside the teenager, who eventually revived and shared his story. The young man explained that he had been walking along State Route 95, where it intersects with Elm Street, when he encountered Huggin' Molly, a towering figure who hovered over him and blocked his path, refusing to let him pass. Terrified, the teen had bolted, running past the cemetery and the old school, only to collide with the side of the Clenney house in the darkness, knocking himself senseless.

The mystery of Huggin' Molly's true identity drips with unease like a whisper carried on a cold southern wind. No one knows for sure who—or what—she really was. Some say she was once a grieving mother, driven mad by the loss of her only child, doomed to wander the streets in eternal mourning. Others claim she was a woman wronged in life—murdered or betrayed—and now stalks the night, her twisted soul fueled by sorrow and silent rage.

Her legend has woven itself into the very bones of Abbeville, Alabama. They say she appears after nightfall, a towering figure cloaked in black, her footsteps muffled by the darkness. Children who stay out past curfew have claimed to see her silhouette at the edge of the lamplight—tall, shadowy, unmoving. Then, with a terrifying swiftness, she closes the distance.

She doesn't speak. She doesn't scream. She only hugs—tight and suffocating, bone-crushing and cold. Her embrace paralyzes, and then, just when the child thinks the air has left their lungs for good, she leans in and screams—a long, high-pitched wail that echoes in their ears for days. But when others come running, there's nothing there. Only a trembling child and the faint scent of something old and forgotten.

Parents in Abbeville still whisper the warning as dusk creeps in: "Be home before dark... or Huggin' Molly will find you."

And though it's said to scare misbehaving children, even grown folk lock their doors a little earlier than usual. Because in the quiet stretch of night, under the heavy hush of southern trees, you just might hear footsteps following yours... and feel arms reaching through the dark.

Alaska
Something Ancient Moves in Darkness

The Alaska Triangle is a vast and chilling region stretching between Anchorage, Juneau, and Utqiagvik. It is not just infamous—it is feared. Since the early 1970s, over 20,000 people have vanished within its icy borders without a trace. No calls for help. No wreckage. No remains. Just... gone.

One of the most unnerving disappearances happened on January 26, 1950. A U.S. Air Force C-54 Skymaster, tail number 2469, lifted off from Anchorage with 44 people on board, bound for Montana. It was dusk. The temperature was bitter. The sky was unforgiving. The plane simply vanished.

No emergency signal. No crash site. Despite massive search efforts, not a single clue was ever found. It was as if the aircraft had been swallowed whole by the sky.

Many blame the brutal elements—the wilderness, the cold, the unpredictable terrain. But the Indigenous Tlingit people have told a different story for centuries. They speak of creatures that walk between worlds, ancient forces not bound by logic or time.

One such entity is Kushtaka, or Kóoshdaa káa—the land otter man. A shapeshifter. A predator of the soul. Kushtaka are said to hunt in pairs, luring victims to their doom by mimicking human voices—especially the cries of lost children. Once a person follows the sound, they're often never seen again. Some are torn apart. Others are transformed into Kushtaka themselves, forever trapped, their souls denied the chance to reincarnate.

Further south, in Thomas Bay, the stories grow darker still. Known as the Bay of Death after a devastating landslide killed hundreds in 1750, the area earned a new nickname from early prospectors: "Devil's Country." In the early 1900s, those who entered often came back changed—*if* they came back at all from the godforsaken place.

In 1898, a 17-year-old miner named Harry Colp arrived in the area. A few years later, in 1900, Colp and three companions—Charlie, John, and Fred—heard rumors of gold near the Patterson River. Charlie was the first to scout the location alone, taking enough supplies for three months. But he returned just weeks later, wild-eyed, exhausted, and shaken. He brought a chunk of quartz flecked with gold but refused to talk about it. Not at first.

When pressed, Charlie finally told them the truth. After setting up camp, he climbed a ridge to scout the land. What he saw froze him in place:

"—the most hideous creatures I had ever seen. I couldn't describe them as anything but devils; they were neither men nor monkeys, yet they resembled both. They were entirely sexless, with bodies covered in long, coarse hair—except where scabs and running sores took their place. They clawed at the air, trying to reach me. Their cries filled the air. The smell from their bodies... it made me sick."

His gun, broken earlier, was useless. Charlie ran. Their clawed hands scraped at his skin as he fled through the woods and into his canoe.

The others scoffed at Charlie's tale—until John and Fred made their own journey. Not long after, they returned broken, pale, and eerily quiet. Fred left quickly, but before he did, he confided in Colp: A creature had sat on the bow of his boat, forcing him to paddle without rest. Every time he stopped, it whispered something low and unintelligible.

John stayed behind long enough to tell Colp about Fred's descent into madness. At one point, Fred dropped to all fours and began biting at the bark of a small jack pine, barking like an animal. He swore the devil creatures were still after them.

Colp would return to Thomas Bay several times but never saw the creatures himself. Still, the area pulsed with an uneasy energy, and the stories never stopped.

During a heavy snowstorm in August 1925, a trapper set his lines near the Muddy River. One night, he heard his dog howl and then fall silent. The next morning, the dog was gone. In the snow, the trapper found its prints—alongside something else. Something bigger. The prints looked part bear, part barefoot human, but...wrong. Unnatural. He followed the trail until suddenly, the dog's tracks ended mid-stride—just stopped. As if it had been lifted into the sky. The trapper, unnerved but determined, followed the other prints.

Hours passed. Then he realized he had walked in a complete circle, right back to where the dog's tracks had ended. Something had been leading him. Watching him.

He shared the prints with a local farmer who couldn't explain them. Three weeks later, the trapper vanished. No body. No clue. Just more silence added to the growing void of the Triangle.

Something ancient moves in the darkness of the Alaska Triangle, stealing bodies, stealing souls. It doesn't just hunt. It waits. And it never leaves empty-handed.

Arizona
The Fall of Leone Jenson

In the heart of downtown Phoenix stands the San Carlos Hotel, its elegant façade a timeless reminder of another era. Opened in 1928, it was once the pinnacle of modern luxury in the Southwest—boasting ornate Italian-inspired architecture, air conditioning, steam heat, and indoor plumbing, a rarity at the time. It promised comfort, prestige... and something else.

At approximately 2:45 a.m. on May 7, 1928, a patron at the San Carlos Hotel heard a scream. Riding his bike down a dark street nearby, Merchant Patrolman George also heard the cry.

It was followed by a heavy thud. He then steered his bike toward the source of the sounds, where he arrived upon the crushed and grotesquely bent body of a young woman lying dead on the pavement of Monroe Street.

The 32-year-old woman, Leone Jenson, had been staying at the hotel for two days in a third-floor room of the seven-floor building. She had fair skin and bobbed blonde hair, and at the time of her death, she was dressed in a thin, rose-colored dress, light shoes, and stockings. She also wore a light tan coat and a matching hat. It was believed that she had been holding the hat in her hand during her final moments, as it was neither soiled nor crushed when her body was discovered.

One hour before her jump, she wrote several letters dated "1:15 a.m., Monday," approximately ninety minutes before the scream was heard. The three letters were composed on stationery from the San Carlos Hotel. At the same time, a separate note was hastily scribbled on telegraph blanks, making it difficult to read.

The notes would reveal a story that the dead woman could not share—she was likely sent to Arizona for the dry air, which doctors believed assisted in the treatment of lung diseases such as tuberculosis. But weakening from her ailment and with little money, she felt all hope was lost. And it was.

To the undertaker from Phoenix, she wrote: "Nervous breakdown; here for lung trouble; too weak to walk; lost appetite; doctors make me sick—have had too many. Just another lonesome and ill stranger."

To the undertaker from Los Angeles, she wrote:

"My burden was more than I could carry, so am coming 'back home' in the way I predicted, but not as a suicide. But this long living agony is too much for me—and now having suffered a nervous breakdown, I could never go through with it. Am too weak to walk and all in all, I am through.

Here are a few of my last requests. Bury me in my tan dress and high-heeled slippers. Organ music above all things. And can you arrange for two girls to sing as I have always loved harmony, 'Nearer My God To Thee' if there is one—and some other one which I wish you to select. Need a Marcel (soft wave hairstyle made by heated curling iron), and my nails are terrible, but have been too sick to care for anything. Goodbye and good luck. Think of me kindly. Miss Leone Jenson."

To the Hotel Manager, written on the back of an envelope of the Pan Carlos hotel, and was found with another short note in Miss Jensen's purse, which was tightly clutched in her fist when she was discovered on the sidewalk pavement below, **she wrote:** "The coroner will attend to my bill and be sure all my clothes are packed, as all wearing apparel is known when it arrives in Los Angeles. I have five dollars, which he will get later on tonight. Will that help any? My income was due the 10th, but it wasn't to be." The second note, a rather rambling affair, bade a general goodbye to her friends and ended with the line, "Darn this hotel pen."

She is long dead but not gone. As with ghosts and certain tragedies, her spirit lingers long after. When considering the desire to see a ghost, it's essential to reflect on the varying rationales behind this urge. Some individuals experience an intense fascination with the supernatural; however, upon encountering the dead, many often wish they had not pursued that experience. Please keep this in mind if you decide to seek out Leone Jenson, as others have had this experience— Imagine as you step into the dimly lit lobby of the hotel, a shiver courses down your spine. The air is thick with an unsettling silence, broken only by the soft tap of shoes on the floor. You can almost taste the bitterness of regret that seems to cling to the walls, steeped in the stories of those who have come and gone.

You make your way to the seventh floor, each step echoing like a heartbeat in the stillness, your pulse quickening as you near your destination. The flickering fluorescent lights overhead cast long shadows that dance along the corridor, and the chill in the air wraps around you like a shroud. It's as if the building itself is holding its breath, waiting. Watching. Leering.

As you pause, a sudden cold breeze rushes past, carrying a faint whisper, a ghostly sigh that implores you to leave. Your heart hammers in your chest, yet your curiosity pulls you forward. The door creaks open, revealing a room untouched by time yet suffocated in an inexplicable sadness.

You feel it then—a presence behind you, heavy and sorrowful. Turning slowly, you catch a glimpse of her: Leone Jenson! Her ethereal form flickers in and out of existence, a haunting silhouette draped in a light tan coat that flows like mist. Her eyes, hollow and filled with despair, stare through you as if searching for something lost among the remnants of her tragic end.

With a sudden gasp, she vanishes, and the air grows colder. The lingering feeling of her presence remains, thickening the atmosphere with deep, intense despair. You can almost hear her sobs echoing in your mind like a distant memory begging to be acknowledged. The darker the corridor grows, the more you sense her turmoil—her torment reaching out to you, igniting a suffocating dread. It grabs you. Now, that agonizing turmoil is yours.

As you retreat, finally escaping the haunted space, the chill follows you, an uninvited reminder of sorrow that clings to your skin, a touch of the otherworldly that may never leave you. To step into the world once more feels like a betrayal to the pain that lingers here, a sorrowful melody that refuses to fade into silence. You go. But those feelings never, ever leave.

Arkansas
Post Oak Ghost

The Ozarks have always worn a shroud of mystery—deep forests, tangled hollows, and scattered, whispering settlements that seem untouched by time. In its earlier days, when isolation reigned, and the wild still held sway, only the hardiest of souls dared to settle there. One such place lay hidden between the dark waters of War Eagle Stream and the winding King's River, a quiet patch of land known as Post Oak Gap.

Though no Post Oak trees remain there today, one once stood, gnarled and looming—its limbs crooked like the fingers of a corpse. The tree was already ancient when the land saw its newest settler. Weathered. Watching.

The locals had long avoided it, crossing the road when passing by, muttering prayers beneath their breath. They said something clung to that tree—something old and restless. Whispers of a curse. Shadows were seen hanging between its limbs at twilight. There was a coldness in the air, no matter the season. And sometimes, when a back was turned, its gnarled limbs seemed to twist and stretch like skeletal hands—reaching, grasping, as if aching to drag someone into its cold, wooden embrace, never to be seen again.

Its story, as they say, goes like this:

In the 1880s, a young family named Sedar and Iona Bush moved to the area from Kentucky and built a log cabin on the flatlands a few miles from Post Oak Gap. They cleared the surrounding land using a plow and a horse and fenced it in with wooden rails. Behind their little cabin stood a giant tree, a Post Oak, which was formed by two trees growing together at the trunk and base, with their limbs spreading out in opposite directions. The settlers left it standing, knowing its large canopy would provide shade from the summer sun. That autumn, a baby girl was born, and they named her Hazel because her brown eyes resembled the hazelnuts they gathered in October.

As the child grew, those passing by the homestead often saw the little girl playing beneath the tree's canopy. They shuddered, but no one warned the young couple about the uneasy sense that clung to the tree—the heavy, unspoken belief that it was cursed. Perhaps they remained silent out of fear, or perhaps they hoped it was only superstition. But deep down, they all knew better.

So Sedar and Iona Bush were unaware of the shadows creeping ever closer. However, the chilling truth loomed just beyond their awareness: they should have been afraid.

Hazel would frequently climb the branches and sit in the fork between the two trunks, eventually drifting off to sleep in its gentle embrace. Later, she would get up and call out from her little hidey-hole, "Mama, come find me!" Iona would pretend to search high and low. As the little girl's giggles grew louder, Mama would finally discover her with a playful scold. "Oh, dear child, there you are!" Iona would say. "Where have you been for so long, my darling daughter? I thought I'd never find you." Mama teased her little one as she climbed down from the tree, and she tickled Hazel until the girl burst out laughing. It was their favorite game, the hiding game, and they played it every night.

One day, while playing near the tree at the age of three, the child discovered a gold nugget. She eagerly brought it to her mother, holding it out in her chubby palm. Iona gasped when she recognized it as a gold nugget and urged the girl to show her where she found it. Excitedly, she called her husband, and together, they searched beneath the tree, discussing the possibility of panning through the dirt for more nuggets. However, their excitement dimmed as farm duties awaited, and the discovery was soon forgotten as winter approached.

Nearly a year later, Sedar hammered the little nugget into a tiny band ring for Hazel's birthday. He carefully etched her name, "HAZEL," along the rim. The little girl hugged the ring and wiggled it on her finger, so pleased with the gift that she never took it off.

One afternoon the following summer, Sedar was working in the field beneath the hot sun. Occasionally, he would stop to wipe the sweat from his brow and glance upward, wishing for rain. Iona was enthusiastically canning huckleberries.

The humid air pressing down on her made her short-tempered. Little Hazel wasn't feeling well that day and began tugging at her mother's dress while mewling for attention. "I want to play the hiding game, Mama," she told Iona petulantly. Frustrated, Iona lost her temper, spanked her child, and snapped, "Go play and leave me alone."

Little Hazel began to sob in despair, telling her mama that she would go away and never come back. With those words hanging in the air, the child ran off. Iona continued her work, forgetting about Hazel's tantrum for the moment. Then, suddenly, the ground began to shake violently. The cabin swayed and shook, and branches and trees surrounding them began to fall and crash as the earth trembled from some underground disturbance.

Iona instinctively called out for Hazel, but when there was no response, she started searching for the little girl. Iona hurried to the cabin and stumbled over several branches that had fallen from the large oak tree where Hazel usually sat. However, Hazel was nowhere to be found.

By this time, Sedar had returned from the field. Hearing his wife's screams, he found Iona in a state of hysteria, frantically rummaging through the brush in search of their daughter. Sedar quickly joined the desperate search, along with neighbors who had been notified. The search area expanded to include the surrounding hills and hollows as Iona recalled her child saying she was going far away and would never come home. Despite everyone's efforts, no trace of Hazel was found, and no clue about the missing child's whereabouts emerged.

Over time, the search parties dwindled, with most people trying to believe that a wild animal roaming the woods had taken her away. The child had vanished. But those who were laughed at when they spoke of the curse in earlier years were eager to rub it in to those who scoffed at their doubts.

Despite this, they continued to conceal their suspicions from the parents even as the years passed.

Twenty-five years later, Iona had aged significantly more than most people her age, and the years of grief over losing her little girl had taken a heavy toll. She was dying, and friends and family had gathered by her bedside in the main room of her little cabin, awaiting the moment. A storm loomed on the horizon, with lightning flashing across the sky and wind howling through the cracks between the windows and panes.

At night, the sleepy visitors were startled from their silent watch when a child's soft voice echoed from just outside the cabin. It seemed to rise from the depths of the forest. One visitor's eyes widened, and he whispered in the tense silence, "It's a ghost." Thunder rumbled, and rain pelted hard against the roof. Was it merely the wind? Those inside held their breath, and again, the soft voice called out, this time a bit louder and closer. However, none of them, frozen in their seats, could make out the words. The somber tone shifted to one of anxiety as the voice called out again, louder and much nearer as if it were right at the worn-out front door.

"Mama, come find me!" the otherworldly voice cried out. "Mama!" The dying woman wheezed and panted, saying, "Hazel! Open the door, Sedar; it's Hazel!" Those inside were paralyzed with fear, their eyes darting to Sedar, whose mouth had fallen open in shock. Then, as if snapped out of a trance, Sedar rushed to the cabin door and flung it wide open.

A blast of frigid wind rushed in, and lightning streaked across the sky. The gust extinguished the lamps, plunging the room into darkness. Nothing stood at the threshold—no ghost, no child—only the night, intermittently illuminated by flashes of lightning. But the gnarled branches of the old cursed tree thrashed angrily, frantically, and violently, like arms reaching into the sky to catch a kerchief lost in the wind.

Sedar quickly shut the door against the rain, and the lamps were lit. The room fell silent momentarily as no one dared to mention the strange occurrence. Then the dying woman gasped and called in a weak voice: "Hazel, where are you?" The soft words startled those present, slicing through the thick, heavy air like a sharp knife. "Oh, dear child, there you are!" Iona huffed, her voice breaking. "Where have you been for so long, my darling daughter? I thought I'd never find you." And as the storm raged outside, Iona Bush took her last breath.

As dawn broke, the storm finally began to subside, and some of those who had gathered around Iona's deathbed stepped outside to stretch their legs. They quickly noted that the old Post Oak tree had been struck by lightning, splitting it in half with the two trunks now broken apart.

Sedar stepped outside and curiously inspected the tree stump. Among the splintered trunks, he discovered an old bronze sign that had been tacked long ago, reading "POST OAK GAP." As he cleared away brush from the remaining stump, he noticed a flash of white and decided to investigate further. He peered inside and brushed away some pieces of old cloth and debris with his palm, and he uncovered a child's bones. He felt something small and metallic when he gently poked at them with his finger. With trembling fingers, Sedar picked up a tiny gold band and saw "HAZEL" engraved on it.

On the day she disappeared, little Hazel, overwhelmed by the sorrows children often feel, ran to her safe place—the old tree fork—and sat between its two massive trunks. As the earth shook, the two trees sprang apart from each other. It caused the child to fall into the hollow inside. They then snapped back together, trapping little Hazel until she perished, only to be discovered many years later. A lightning strike revealed the old tree's secret and freed the child it had held in its deathly embrace.

Mother and child were buried together, united at last—but only in death. The old tree has long since rotted away, its gnarled trunk lost to time. Yet something lingers. When the wind howls through Post Oak Gap, it carries more than leaves and dust. It also scatters its seeds into the wind, spreading the curse that the old oak possessed. Some say the dead rise with the gusts, riding on the cursed breath of that long-vanished tree. In the stillness, if you listen closely, a child's voice drifts on the breeze: "Mama, come find me..." And then, softer still, comes the reply—warped and distant, as though spoken from the cold earth itself: "Oh, dear child... there you are. Where have you been for so long, my darling daughter? I thought I'd never find you."

But what was once a reunion of love now sounds more like a warning.

California
An Unhappy Ghost

In the late 1800s, a narrow-gauge railroad track in Alameda, California, was part of the South Pacific Coast Railroad. It was a route used often and familiar to those along its path. It ran 80 miles from Alameda to Santa Cruz, with a ferry connection from Alameda to San Francisco. The trains sped along the tracks, the shrill wail of wheels on steel and the blare of horns echoing their familiar cry. One section featured a bend in the railroad tracks near Sherman Street in Alameda. This curve was necessary due to the constraints imposed by the nearby streets and properties, and many times, the impatient engineers barely slowed down as they rushed through to reach their next stop on time. They should have—

It was quite a ride for those inside, sometimes jolting passengers in various directions. Most were aware of the curve and held tightly to something for support, like children gripping the safety bar on a roller coaster as it peaks at a high hill, preparing to plunge down the dizzying drop. However, some individuals were unaware of the heart-jolting curve, resulting in a mortifying experience. They were also oblivious to the peculiar ghost that haunted the area due to this twist in the train's path.

It wasn't a well-kept secret, though few would openly admit to seeing the ghostly figure after dark. Those rail workers who labored on the tracks at night were given warnings, often dismissed as mere hearsay or the delusions of those who feared things that go bump in the night.

Thomas Schoepf, a level-headed employee, was hired as a night watchman for the central section of Almeda around 1899, which included the Sherman Street Curve. As a new worker, he received training from Policeman Dennis Welch, who provided him with the details of his position. Before departing after the training, Welch paused, his tone darkening with a shadow of something unspoken. "Oh, and by the way," he added, almost as an afterthought, "some of the guys say there's a ghost out there—one that doesn't rest easy. They say it stumbles along the tracks once a year... still searching for what it lost. Just... make sure you're not around when it does."

Schoepf was no novice; he had previously worked in jobs where older employees tried to scare new hires with outlandish and frightening stories. Even seasoned night shift workers, known for their fearlessness in the dark and who often laughed at whimsical tales, sometimes felt a wave of dread when they ventured into the night. In certain locations, they couldn't help but conjure vexing images in their minds.

You see, the apparition—gruesome beyond words—emerged from the shadows like a waking nightmare. It was dressed in the tattered remains of a soldier's uniform, a rusted bugle swinging gently from one shoulder, whispering ghost-notes into the wind. But where his head should have been, there was only a ragged stump, a raw, nubby lump of flesh and bone. The phantom moved with a slow, deliberate rhythm along the curved stretch of track, pacing as though bound by some cursed ritual. In one decayed, skeletal hand, it clutched a basket—what lay inside, no one could say. And yet, those who have seen it swear they could hear the faint sound of wheezing breath as if the thing still hoped—still hunted—for the piece of itself it would never find.

In the long hours before dawn, when the world holds its breath and even the air feels uneasy, the old stories start to claw their way to the surface. Whispers passed between night patrolmen, dismissed as drunken talk or the mutterings of men too long alone in the dark. But not all of them laughed.

Schoepf shared his account with a San Francisco Examiner reporter in 1896, his voice measured, yet edged with something colder than doubt: "When I first commenced my work, Policeman Dennis Welch told me the story of the headless ghost. Of course, I laughed at him. Welch told me the ghost always appeared on the anniversary of the boy's death—August 15." He paused before continuing. "Curiosity, more than anything else, prompted me to look for the ghost on that night three years ago. The apparition frightened me then, but I have seen it twice since without being scared in the least."

Schoepf's words grew heavier, as if weighed down by what he'd seen. "Shortly after 1 o'clock, the ghost appears. I saw it this morning quite plainly. From how that restless spirit paced back and forth, I believe it was searching for that missing head."

Each year, like clockwork, the thing rises—its presence staining the air with dread, walking the curve of the track as if trapped in the moment of its own violent end. And always, always looking. Most believed this ghost to be that of James Fallon, a young bugler for the National Guard. On August 1, 1886, he was traveling with his regiment, returning from the annual camp at Santa Cruz. While standing on the platform of a train car as it sped through Alameda, the train swung around the sharp curve at Sherman Street. He was thrown from the vehicle and lay there, stunned. It was dusk, and the engineer could not see him, and the train ran over the unconscious soldier and cut his head from his body. A policeman found the corpse, but the head was never located, most likely crushed and carried away by the train.

James Fallon returns, his footsteps slow, deliberate, and unnatural. The reek of decay follows. He carries a basket in his hands, its woven sides creaking with each movement, waiting to be filled with his moldering head with wisps of hair barely clinging to its scalp, dark pits where eyes once rotted away, and a flap of parched skin where his nose once lay.

He stops occasionally, kneels, and begins to grovel along the old track bed. One decayed arm stretches forward, trembling with unnatural life, while four blackened, rotting fingers drag across the ground—patting, groping, clawing through the cold stones like a blind thing in agony. The nails screech against the earth, peeling and cracking as they scrape. Nothing. No relief. No release.

He rises—bones snapping with the motion, headless shoulders jerking in twitching defiance. He staggers along the abandoned tracks, swaying like a broken puppet, only to collapse again with a sickening thud. On his knees, he digs, moans low and hollow from a throat that no longer breathes.

Again. And again.

Each movement is a desperate act, a cursed ritual—searching, always searching—for the head ripped from his body long ago. And he will keep searching, night after night, until someone... or something... puts an end to his torment.

Colorado
Colorado Cannibal

A grim and unsettling tale haunts the remote wilderness of Colorado—one that begins with a drifter named Alferd Packer. After his discharge from the military—where he suffered frequent epileptic seizures during the Civil War—Packer wandered from one job to the next. He tried his hand at hunting, mining, and teamster work, but those who crossed his path quickly learned he was a man ill-suited for such pursuits. He got lost easily, was known to stretch the truth beyond recognition, and his foul temper often turned to confrontation.

Whispers followed him like shadows. He was a thief, many claimed—someone to be watched when backs were turned. A man who stirred unease around campfires and whose presence could sour the mood of any expedition.

Driven by greed and desperation, he made his way to Colorado, lured by the promise of gold glimmering beneath the snow-choked mountains. But what Packer would eventually find in those remote hills was not fortune... but infamy.

In 1873, when Packer was 31 years old, he joined a group of prospectors heading through Utah to the San Juan Mountains in Colorado. He claimed to be an experienced guide familiar with the San Juan territory. Lacking provisions, he offered to guide the group for twenty-five dollars, and they accepted his offer out of necessity. Early in the journey, the travelers found Packer lazy and stubborn, often quarreling and greedily hoarding the rationed food for himself. As supplies dwindled, they were forced to feed on horse food while heavy snowfall accumulated along the Spanish Trail, which connected Santa Fe, New Mexico, to Los Angeles, California.

In mid-January 1874, they struggled into camp with Chief Ouray, a friendly Ute leader near Montrose, Colorado. He provided them with food and warned them against crossing the mountains in winter, inviting them to stay in his camp until spring. Originally consisting of 21 men, the party suffered greatly during the harsh winter. Only six men remained by February 9, 1874, including Packer: George Noon, Israel Swan, James Humphrey, Frank Miller, and Shannon Wilson Bell. Despite Chief Ouray's warnings about the dangers of winter travel in the mountains, they chose to leave his camp.

On April 16, 1874, Packer emerged alone from the wilderness at the Los Piños Indian Agency near Saguache.

He claimed that his companions had abandoned him after he suffered from frozen feet. However, suspicions began to arise, as he appeared to be in remarkably good health despite having gone without food for two months. Where had the missing men from his group gone?

Under questioning by General Adams at the agency, Packer confessed to eating them for survival. He claimed that one by one, his companions had died from starvation or exposure and that he had eaten their flesh to survive.

Part of Packer's statement included:

"I, Alfred Packer, desire to make true and voluntary statement in regard to the occurrences in Southern Colorado during the winter of 1873 - 1874. . . Swan asked me to go up and find out whether I could see something from the mountains. . . When I came back to camp after being gone nearly all day I found the redheaded man [Bell] who acted crazy in the morning sitting near the fire roasting a piece of meat which he had cut out of the leg of the German butcher [Miller] the latter's body was lying the furthest off from the fire down the stream, his skull was crushed in with the hatchet. The other three men were lying near the fire, they were cut in the forehead with the hatchet some had two some three cuts –I came within a rod of the fire, when the man saw me, he got up with his hatchet towards me when I shot him sideways through the belly, he fell on his face, the hatchet fell forwards. I grabbed it and hit him in the top of the head—I went back to the fire covered the men up and fetched the piece of meat that was near the fire. I made a new fire near my camp and cooked the piece of meat and ate it. I tried to get away every day but could not, so I lived off the flesh of these men, the bigger part of the 60 days I was out. . ." I, Al Packer, of my own free will and voluntarily do swear that the above statement is true, the whole truth and nothing but the truth.

So help me God (s) Alferd Packer Subscribed and sworn before me this 16th day of March A.D., 1883 Sim. W. Cantril Notary Public.

His story shifted with every retelling, but the truth eventually clawed its way to the surface. Lies became half-truths. Half-truths became confessions soaked in blood. When the search party reached the base of Slumgullion Pass, they didn't find lost hikers—they found remains. Scattered bones. Torn flesh. Signs of slaughter and consumption. The wilderness had not taken them. He had. Though charged with murder, he dodged the noose. Instead, the court gave him forty years for manslaughter, as if that word could soften what he'd done. He served eighteen and emerged with a name that chilled the spine of anyone who heard it: the Colorado Cannibal.

If there's any wisdom to scrape from a story like this, it's buried beneath fear: don't let the devil into your camp. Especially not the one who comes alone, with no name worth checking and eyes that never blink long enough to see remorse. And if you find yourself stranded in the dead of winter, miles from anything human, surrounded by those who smile too easily while rations disappear—remember this: the first to act often survives.

If you can't do what Packer did... pray the one who can doesn't get hungry first.

Connecticut
Annabelle

In 1970, a young student nurse named Donna received what seemed like an innocent gift from her mother an old Raggedy Ann doll. Its stitched cotton body, stuffed limbs, and innocent, childlike appearance initially appeared harmless. Red yarn hair framed its pale face, its button eyes staring vacantly at the world, and its mouth was stitched in a permanent, unsettling grin. But there was something about the doll that felt... wrong.

Donna's roommate, Angie, noticed it too. At first, the doll was simply a quirky decoration placed on Donna's bed as a reminder of her childhood. But as days passed, they began to notice disturbing changes. When Donna would leave for work and return, the doll had shifted positions—its limbs were moved, its body turned in unnatural ways. Then, it disappeared from rooms altogether, only to be found in places it shouldn't have been: on the floor, in corners, or even kneeling, as if in prayer. The doll didn't just move; it seemed to have a will of its own.

But that wasn't the worst of it.

Angie discovered a small, crumpled piece of parchment paper hidden under the doll one night. Upon unfolding it, she read a chilling message written in a jagged, almost childlike hand: "Help me." The words seemed to crawl into her very soul as if the paper itself were alive with some malignant presence. They had no parchment paper in their apartment—none that looked like this. And the messages didn't stop there. More notes appeared over the following days, with phrases like "Help us" and a cryptic plea: "Help Lou."

Terrified, the two women were pushed to their limits, and in desperation, they reached out to a medium. What followed was a séance that would unlock horrors none of them could have foreseen. The medium's voice trembled as she spoke of a seven-year-old girl named Annabelle who had died in tragic circumstances and whose restless spirit now clung to the doll. The medium claimed the doll was simply a vessel for Annabelle's sorrowful soul, seeking peace. But something wasn't right.

Soon, the presence that had latched onto the doll began to reveal its true nature. The more Donna and Angie tried to ignore the doll, the more it demanded attention. The simple fabric toy began to emanate an oppressive, malevolent energy.

The air around it grew thick with a sense of dread. The doll's innocent smile turned into something mocking, its eyes gleaming with an unholy light. And then, the blood began to appear.

Red stains—deep, dark crimson, the color of fresh blood—soaked into the doll's fabric, spreading like a stain from the inside. It was no longer a mere toy. It was something darker, something dangerous.

In a final act of terror, Donna and Angie reached out to Ed and Lorraine Warren, the famed paranormal investigators. Upon their examination, the Warrens quickly dismissed the idea of a benign spirit and came to a chilling conclusion: the doll wasn't haunted by a child's ghost at all. It was an unholy vessel—a demonic entity pretending to be Annabelle, seeking to possess the living.

The Warrens took the doll, but not to restore it to peace. They locked it away in a glass case at their occult museum, the warning clear: DO NOT OPEN. The case was adorned with signs of protection, but the whispers of the cursed doll continued to echo in the dark corners of their museum. The séance had unwittingly invited a force far more sinister than anyone could have imagined—a force that would never rest until it claimed a new host.

And the Raggedy Ann doll remained, its stitched smile still intact, staring out from the glass—waiting.

Delaware
Quaker Bonwell's Old Fence Rail Dog

In the late 1700s, Mary and Michael Hall Bonwell acquired a house and a vast stretch of land near Andrews Lake, west of Frederica in what is now Delaware. It seemed like a promising start—Bonwell, the only builder of grist and sawmills south of Wilmington, was already gaining recognition for his work. His property, which eventually became known as Leamington Mills, included a bark mill—a place where the earth itself seemed to groan under the weight of the tasks it was forced to bear.

At this mill, oak and hemlock trees were stripped of their bark with a quiet, unsettling efficiency. The tannin-rich bark, ground into a fine powder, became tanbark—its primary purpose to treat and transform raw animal hides into leather.

But there was something about the place. The grinding of the bark, the smell of earth and decay, the constant hum of machinery—it was all too perfect, too precise. The air around the mill, thick with dampness, whispered of things best left forgotten. And as the years went by and the mill aged, the land seemed to slowly close in, hiding secrets, the trees growing darker, the shadows deeper. And Bonwell himself seemed to be falling into that decay, becoming more aggressive. Angrier. More violent.

Although the Bonwells viewed it merely as a business, it was much more—a dark, silent trade with the very land itself. And it would seem that the land demanded a price, a price not yet paid.

An old story comes from the area of "Quaker Bonwell" and the tannery. Bonwell was notorious for his quick and vicious temper, standing over his workers with an iron fist. For the young and those whose tiny fingers were not swift enough to keep up, he would erupt into a furious tirade and thrash them soundly.

One day, he was angry with a young Black boy who worked hard in his mills but struggled to keep up with the adult workers. Bonwell beat him to death and tossed the child into the bark mill, disposing of the corpse by grinding it up. Although the boy's sad and gruesome demise was known around the community, it went unpunished by local authorities at the time.

According to legend, Bonwell was so cruel and despised that when he died, his white neighbors refused to have anything to do with him and would not bury his body.

Members of the Black community felt a responsibility to ensure that his restless spirit would not roam freely. If he could cause chaos and commit murder without remorse during his life, then surely, in an unearthly form, he could unleash even greater horrors after death. They decided to give him a Christian burial. But the old man would just not lay.

Bonwell returned from the dead shortly after being buried. He took on the form of a demon-like black dog, resembling a hellhound. The creature's presence was a terror that clung to the land, stalking the roads and haunting the night with an unrelenting malice. It was a massive, shadowy dog—its form twisted and unnatural, a hulking figure that would appear out of nowhere along Route 12, west of Frederica. Its eyes gleamed with a predatory hunger, and it terrorized anyone who dared to cross its path. Horses panicked at its approach, rearing and galloping in a frenzy, their riders helpless as the beast surged forward, howling into the night.

Attempts to drive it away were futile. Sticks and rocks thrown in desperation passed through its form, clattering to the ground with eerie finality. The creature wasn't just a beast—it was something far darker, something supernatural that couldn't be touched or harmed. Its foul reek resembled something two days dead beneath a summer sky, stinking of rot and decay.

The Fence Rail Dog, or Quaker Bonwell's Old Long Dog, as it came to be known, would appear without warning, dashing past travelers at terrifying speeds. Its ghostly form was a blur, its presence a warning of impending doom that sent shivers down the spines of those who saw it. And yet, there are still whispers today—tales from witnesses who have seen its form flash before their eyes, a nightmarish apparition that races through the night like a predator still hunting, still waiting for its next victim.

Florida
The Ghost That Would Not Go Away

In the 1880s, Palatka, Florida, a thriving town at the crossroads of commerce, became a place where shadows seemed to stretch longer than the daylight for those who lived and worked on its darker streets. Its location along the St. Johns River made it a transportation hub, bustling with steamboats and railroads. However, as its fortunes rose, so did the darkness that clung to its streets. Crime surged like a creeping disease, infecting the very soul of the town, and law enforcement found itself drowning in a tide of chaos.

For the men who wore the badge, it wasn't just the criminals they feared. The streets were thick with an unsettling presence that gnawed at the edges of their sanity. Each night, they walked under the oppressive weight of unseen eyes, the streets whispering secrets no one dared to speak aloud. Once seen as a necessary duty, the job became an unrelenting nightmare. The eerie silence between crimes only heightened the dread, as though something far worse than thieves and outlaws was lurking just beyond the veil of the ordinary.

Some policemen who patrolled the narrow, dimly lit streets began to crack under the pressure. The weight of it all—the constant fear, the ominous tension that seemed to hang in the air—was too much to bear. It wasn't just the endless stream of crime or the palpable menace in the breeze. It was something more, something darker.

The worst of it, though, was the ones who couldn't take it. They didn't disappear. They lingered, walking the streets with a glazed look in their eyes as if they were still chasing something—or being chased. They were never the same after that final patrol, broken in ways that could never be undone.

Palatka, a place of promise for most, would, for others, become a town where the only certainty was the inevitable descent into madness for those who dared to confront its dark heart. The town's history would forever echo the stories of one policeman who could not escape the burden of its shadows.

In August 1884, John Jackson was a 42-year-old Black police officer serving on the Palatka police force for four years. He was well-respected for his quiet and thoughtful demeanor. One Sunday, he completed his tasks at work and then went home, where he informed his sick wife that he was leaving her. She responded that if he wanted to move, she would sell the house, pack her bags, and gladly go with him.

However, he shook his head and said, "I don't want to leave in that way." He retrieved his gun, lay down on the bed, and declared that he was going to kill himself. After trying to talk her husband out of using the weapon, she finally got up and began to leave the room. As she reached the door, a gunshot rang out, and the man had killed himself instantly with a ball through the heart.

John was buried, and after some time, his wife remarried, and the family moved away. However, the dead policeman did not rest. No tenants seemed to stay in the little house for long; they moved out quickly without much explanation. A few hinted at the presence of a ghost that "made a terrible racket." Several families had very short stays, and the last one fled at midnight, too frightened to return for their furniture the next day. They reported that a gruesome, bloody corpse walked the floors of the house, holding its head and moaning and groaning.

Nearly every form of religious practice was attempted to remove the ghost, ranging from Vodou ceremonies to Catholic rites. Five men entered the house to raise the ghost one night while those living nearby stood outside with lanterns watching. After some time, they felt confident that the ghost had been successfully banished. However, at midnight, those inside began to hear taps on the floor, along the walls, and on the ceiling, like tiny feet walking around the room. Groans and moans soon followed.

The loud explosion of a gunshot echoed through the house, followed by liquid dripping to the floor. The door burst open. A gust of wind nearly toppled the five inside, extinguishing their lanterns. The room was plunged into darkness. The only light came from the open windows, the illuminations of the lanterns lit by curious onlookers outside. It was just enough to reveal an eerie silhouette with a distinct bloody face and skull.

The entity had both hands pressed on the top of its head, holding it against the trunk, and from a gaping hole in the neck, blood flowed in a steady stream down its clothing.

The men stood frozen in place, unable to utter a word until a horrifying, blood-curdling scream echoed from the shadowy figure. Suddenly, those inside sprang into action, rushing out through windows and doors in a panic.

Following that night, the house was left to rot in silence, its windows staring blankly into the void. No one dared step inside, not after the dreadful events that unfolded. The walls, once filled with the sounds of life, now only echoed the whispers of something far darker. Time did not soften the horror; it only deepened it. The house, once a home, became a hollow shell, sinking slowly into neglect as if even the land itself recoiled from what had occurred there.

But the ghost, it seemed, could not be forgotten so easily. It refused to be silenced, its presence lingering like a dark stain on the house. At night, the sound of dragging footsteps would stir the cold, musty air. The creaking of floorboards would echo through the empty halls as if unseen hands were still searching for something that would never be found. It was not content to simply haunt the place; it was angry, vengeful, and relentless.

The foul scent of decay would sometimes waft through the air as though the ghost itself had become part of the house—twisted, rotten, and forever bound to it. Some who dared to come near would report seeing dark figures flicker in the windows, twisted shapes that did not belong to the house. And on the rare nights when the wind howled through the broken glass and long-gone doors, faint, frantic whispers could be heard, always just on the edge of understanding, as if the ghost was speaking to the very walls.

No one could say for sure what it wanted. But those who passed by the forsaken house would swear that sometimes, in the dead of night, they could hear the desperate scratching at the door—louder, more frantic each time, as if the ghost was begging to be let in... or maybe to escape.

Georgia
The Short Life and Long Death of Mary Phagan

Mary Phagan was born into a life of struggle and hardship, her arrival marked by an absence of a father. Her mother, barely managing to scrape by, moved their family to Atlanta in search of a life that would offer a sliver of hope. But hope was a fleeting thing, and it seemed that fate had other plans for the young girl.

At just 10 years old, Mary left school and worked in a textile mill, her small hands learning the rhythm of factory life.

She worked hard, never questioning the weight of her labor, until the day she secured a job at the National Pencil Factory. For 10 cents an hour, she became another cog in the machinery—one of many, insignificant to the eyes of the world. But worse, she would unknowingly walk directly into the mouth of a beast.

For beneath the hum of factory machines and the clinking of metal, something far darker stirred in the shadows. In the corners of that building, in the hidden rooms where eyes seldom wandered, there existed a demon—one that had bided its time in silence, waiting for the right moment. The factory's sterile, industrial atmosphere concealed its hunger. And it was in that very place that Mary would become its prey.

A sinister presence lingered, its teeth sharp and eager, waiting to sink into the flesh of the innocent. There, in the silence of the factory's halls, the beast was ready. Unaware of the danger, Mary was no different from the countless others who worked alongside her until the demon waiting, watching, and always hungry exposed its ugly face.

Those who knew her described 13-year-old Mary Phagan as standing four feet eight inches tall and weighing about 105 pounds. She had reddish-blonde hair and was considered quite beautiful. On April 26, 1913, after having a meal, Mary headed to the National Pencil Company to collect her weekly wages of $1.20 from the manager, 31-year-old Leo Frank. She boarded a streetcar and arrived just after noon, making her way to the second floor, where Leo Frank handed her an envelope containing her pay.

Mary told her mother she was staying to watch the Confederate Memorial Day parade and that she would be home right after. When she did not return home, her family began to search for her frantically, but Mary was nowhere to be found.

On April 27, at approximately 3:00 a.m., Newt Lee, the night watchman of the pencil factory, discovered the body of Mary in the basement. Nearby, he found bloody fingerprints next to a sliding door that led to an alley, suggesting that someone had escaped after her murder. Mary had a cord around her neck. It appeared that she had been assaulted.

Authorities were notified immediately, and suspicions quickly fell on Leo Frank after witnesses reported seeing both Mary and Frank in the building at the same time. Frank, a well-known Jewish-American with a degree in mechanical engineering from Cornell University, was the last person confirmed to have seen her alive when he paid her salary at his office.

Jim Conley, an African American janitor at the factory, provided multiple conflicting statements regarding his involvement and knowledge of the murder. He was arrested shortly after the discovery of Mary's body. Conley attested that he had helped Frank dispose of Mary's body after Frank allegedly killed her, claiming that Frank had asked him to guard the door while he met with Mary.

Conley's testimony was pivotal in securing Frank's conviction despite its inconsistencies and the lack of physical evidence linking Frank to the crime. He offered several contradictory affidavits regarding his involvement and what he claimed to have witnessed on the day of the murder. Conley became a key witness for the prosecution against Frank, stating that Frank had coerced him into covering up the crime by moving the body via elevator to the factory basement, where the police located it the following day.

Leo Frank was put on trial, attracting major media attention and public outrage fueled by anti-Semitic views against him due to his Jewish identity and Northern origins. He was convicted of murder on August 25, 1913.

On August 16 to 17, 1915, a mob from Mary Phagan's hometown of Marietta abducted Leo Frank from the Georgia prison farm in Milledgeville and lynched him near Marietta, Georgia. In 1986, Frank was posthumously pardoned based on dental records that did not match the bite marks found on Mary's body, as well as an admission from 83-year-old Alonzo Mann. At the age of 14, Mann was Frank's assistant and witnessed Jim Conley transporting Mary's body. Mann had been threatened with murder if he reported what he saw.

Following the horrific events, an unsettling darkness began to settle over the city as if the very earth had absorbed the sorrow and horror that had unfolded. Whispers spread like a sickness, tales of a restless presence that refused to stay buried. Locals began to speak of strange occurrences near the site where Mary Phagan's life was violently stolen—an area now marked by the chilling echo of her death. People claimed to hear faint whispers on the wind, as if a voice, too soft to make out, was calling from the depths of the earth itself, yearning for something lost.

On moonless nights, when the streets were empty and the factory sat cold and silent, some swore they could see the faint outline of a figure in white drifting aimlessly near the place where Mary had once worked. Her face, pale and twisted with despair, would appear only momentarily before vanishing into the darkness as though caught between worlds. Witnesses described her as lost, her eyes filled with an unspoken terror, her mouth opening as if to scream—but no sound ever escaped.

It wasn't just Mary. The darkness had claimed both. Leo Frank, too, had left behind a shadow. His lynching had been an act of brutal finality, but reports surfaced that his presence lingered in the place where he met his end. The air would grow inexplicably cold, and the faint sound of footsteps appeared.

Their slow and deliberate pursuit would echo in the dead of night. Some said they could feel a suffocating weight pressing down upon them as if the ground had turned against them, bearing the cursed imprint of a man who never found justice.

At times, people would hear the unmistakable sound of ropes creaking or see the flickering of lights where there should be none. Those who dared to approach the site of Leo Frank's lynching would often report feeling watched, as though unseen eyes were fixed upon them, waiting for something they couldn't name, something they couldn't escape.

The town had changed. It was as if the land itself had become an unwilling vessel, holding the trapped souls of the innocent and the damned. And with every passing year, it seemed the hauntings grew stronger, the figures of Mary and Leo Frank forever cursed to wander the places they had once known, never able to escape the horrors that had sealed their fates by a demon so evil, he escaped justice.

Hawaii
The Wraith in the Thick Grove

Kalaupapa National Historical Park has a dark history. Once a settlement on the northern coast of Moloka'i, Hawaii, it served as a forced colony for people with leprosy, established by King Kamehameha V in the 1860s. The Hawaiian population lacked immunity to many diseases brought to the region, making them particularly vulnerable to infections. In the late 19th century, a number of cases of leprosy emerged in the United States, mainly due to immigration from Turkey, Russia, the Middle East, and Asia, and it subsequently spread to surrounding countries.

Thousands of Hawaiians with leprosy were exiled to Kalaupapa, facing hardship and isolation for over a century. Those who lived there knew about the haunted places within and avoided them at all costs. One particularly eerie area was a densely wooded section along a popular road that remained gloomy and dark even during the day. This overgrown region was primarily bypassed and rarely used; the thick trees muffled the winds, obstructing views of the Kalaupapa cliffs. A distinctive ylang-ylang tree marked the spot where most would stop after dark. The thick trunks and dense foliage blocked views of the cliffs inland, creating an unsettling atmosphere.

Some people dismissed the idea of ghosts as mere superstition, but those who did often paid a heavy price. This area was the site of a murder long ago. In the mid-1900s, a man new to the settlement, unaware of the haunting, drove along this route with his typically obedient dogs in the back seat. As he neared the ylang-ylang tree, his dogs began to bark, snarl, and jump into the front seat. Startled by their reaction, he slammed on the brakes, and just then, he saw a gray, translucent blob that was solid from the shoulders up, partially illuminated by the full moon. Terrified, he quickly backed down the road to a turnaround and returned home.

In the late 1800s, a German doctor served as the physician for the Kalaupapa leprosy settlement. He frequently traveled the route between Kalawao and Kalaupapa during the day to meet boats, examine new patients, and personally hand off outgoing mail to the captains. His mule knew the route well and was typically well-behaved. One evening, as he was returning from Kalawao to attend a concert in Kalaupapa, his patients had left Kalawao early to walk through the grove in daylight. He rode his mule steadily in a hurry, but when they reached the grove's edge, the mule refused to go any further.

After several attempts to persuade it to move, the doctor decided to take a different approach. He rode back a few yards and tried again, but the mule remained stubborn. Frustrated, he turned the mule around and ran it full speed down the trail. Suddenly, the mule came to a dead stop, causing the doctor to fly over its head and land hard on the ground, sustaining head injuries.

Later, patients returning from the concert heard his moans and groans from the woods. Despite the area being known as haunted, three bravely ventured in to investigate. They found both the mule and the injured doctor. The mule still wouldn't move forward, so one of the patients rode it back up the hill while the others assisted the doctor via the bypass trail, bringing him home safely.

A dark legend explains the haunting of the old, forgotten grove, where once stood one of the most beautiful homes on the island—a place now only whispered about by the few who dare venture near. Long ago, when the island had no law or authority, it was where greed and jealousy festered unchecked. A woman cherished for her beauty and kindness lived there in peace, untouched by the dangers of the outside world. But her peace would not last.

A jealous, vengeful soul, consumed by envy, plotted her murder, hoping to claim the home as her own. In the dead of night, with the moon hanging like a pale, watching eye, the woman's life was violently stolen from her. The murderer thought she had won, that the house, the life, and everything the other woman once held dear now belonged to her. But the murderer was gravely mistaken. What followed was far more terrifying than any mortal could bear. The dead woman's wraith, twisted with rage and sorrow, rose from the dark, stained, and desecrated ground. Her ghost was not the peaceful spirit of a departed soul—it was very malevolent.

Her jealousy and fury echoed through the night. She tormented the murderer, pulling the woman into a world of nightmares where the slayer could feel the dead woman's icy fingers brush against her skin and hear her anguished cries in the silence of the rooms.

The tortured soul could not escape the dead woman's unrelenting wrath for nights. Every corner of the house seemed alive with whispers, every shadow hiding the face of a deathless tormentor. The murderer would hear soft, deadly footsteps echoing behind her—closer and closer until she could feel the chill of her presence just behind her neck, ready to drag the cruel, murdering beast into the darkness with her.

The killer, driven mad by the constant terror, could no longer bear it. And in one final act of desperation, the woman took her own life, hoping to escape the torment that had consumed her. But even in death, she was not free.

To this day, the house is nothing more than a rotting shell, and the road that once led to it remains cursed. Some say the woman's wraith still haunts the path, her anguished cries carried on the wind, and her cold gaze searching for another to fall victim to her eternal wrath. Others say the murderer's spirit still lingers, twisted by guilt and madness, trapped in an endless cycle of fear, desperately trying to escape the woman she killed but never quite managing to outrun her.

No one knows which spirit truly haunts that forsaken road. Some hear the soft whisper of a woman weeping in the trees, others catch glimpses of a figure cloaked in shadow, stalking the road in silence. But one thing is certain—whatever haunts that place is restless, filled with a vengeance that can never be satisfied. Those who wander too close might hear a voice on the wind, whispering their name, beckoning them into the same darkness that claimed both of them.

Idaho
The Miner and His Ghostly Mules

Manuel Sato was a solitary miner of rugged independence, traveling with only his mules as company through the wilds north of Boise, Idaho. In the desolate wilderness of Loon Creek, he carried his gold—a treasure he had amassed, so he thought, in secret. One cold morning in 1870, while camping alone in the isolation of Cottonwood Canyon, he built a fire to cook breakfast, the warmth from the flames offering a brief respite from the biting chill.

But as Sato bent over the fire, the shadow of death loomed. A robber, lurking in the forest, advanced swiftly and silently.

Without warning, the man struck, his blade slashing through the morning air, sinking deep into Sato's flesh. The miner fell to the earth, his life spilling out with the gold he carried. In the frenzy of the attack, the murderer, heart racing, failed to unearth the entire fortune hidden nearby. Instead, he fled, leaving Sato's body behind, half-buried under the dirt.

When Sato's body was discovered, it was a grisly scene. A saddlebag containing a portion of his hard-earned gold lay discarded near the fire—its contents still warm with the lingering heat of Sato's last moments. His mules lay dead around him. The soldiers from Fort Boise who came to search for the rest of his treasure never returned with any success. Each time they ventured into the canyon, they were met with an overwhelming sense of dread. Strange, unearthly sounds— low, guttural yowls and mournful moans—echoed through the canyon. Soldiers, once brave and steady, were paralyzed by the eerie noises. Some swore they could hear the rattling of chains and the unmistakable sound of mules braying in the distance, though no pack animals could be seen.

It wasn't just the sounds that terrified them. The very air seemed to thicken with an unnatural weight, the temperature dropping abruptly as if the canyon itself were alive—hunger stirring in the depths of the earth. Some spoke of a shadowy figure they glimpsed on the edges of their vision—Sato's ghost, clad in tattered clothes, still wandering the canyon searching for his lost gold.

But it was the mules that haunted the soldiers the most. Once loyal and docile, the animals had now become twisted specters of their former selves, their cries filled with pain and despair, mingling with Sato's mournful wails. It was as if the spirits of both man and beast were bound together, cursed to wander the canyon forever, seeking what had been stolen from them.

No treasure was ever found. No one dared to return to the area, not after hearing the wails, the rattling chains, and feeling the cold fingers of death brush past them. The legend of Manuel Sato and his cursed treasure endures, a haunting reminder that some places are better left untouched, their dark secrets better left buried. But even now, those who venture too close to Cottonwood Canyon swear they can still hear the echoes of Sato's ghostly calls and the eerie cries of his mules, forever trapped in the hollow of that forsaken land.

Illinois
Death by Murder. Death by Hanging.

Elizabeth "Betsey" Reed was born in the fall of 1807 in Purgatory Swamp, near Palestine, Illinois. The pretty, green-eyed, auburn-haired girl was the youngest of seven children in a penniless farming family. The Fails, her family, struggled against the harsh conditions of their land. In 1815, in a moment of desperate greed, Betsey's mother sold her to a passing peddler in Lawrence County for five pounds of lard and a cast-iron skillet. From that day, the shadows grew darker, swallowing Betsey whole as she walked unknowingly into the waiting jaws of monsters that would consume her.

Betsey endured mistreatment and was sold multiple times over the years before finally managing to escape her captors. As she grew older, she met John Stone at a boarding house where she worked, and the two married. However, their marriage lasted about ten years before he left her under unclear circumstances. Afterward, Betsey returned to Lawrence County and married Leonard Reed in 1842. He was a farmer and trapper who owned a small farm south of Palestine, Illinois, and he was twelve years older than her. Leonard Reed was described as a thin, frail man with salt-and-pepper hair and an oversized nose. He had a perpetual smile and was known for his kind demeanor within the community. The couple lived in a rustic cabin with Leonard's niece, 16-year-old Eveline Deal. They faced many financial hardships, and Betsey's eccentric behavior did not help; she often covered her face with veils due to scars from past injuries.

On August 15, 1844, Leonard Reed's health declined rapidly and he fell severely ill. Many said his downfall followed drinking sassafras tea prepared by Betsey, but most agree that he was a sickly man and his time was due. He died four days later, on August 19, leading to suspicions about the cause of his death. Eveline Deal, Leonard's niece, accused Elizabeth of poisoning Leonard by mixing arsenic into his tea. She claimed to have witnessed Betsey adding the toxin. This accusation gained traction despite the lack of substantial evidence against Elizabeth, other than Eveline's testimony and some circumstantial evidence regarding arsenic found in the home.

Betsey was accused and convicted of murdering her first husband by poisoning him. The trial occurred in Lawrenceville, Illinois, and drew significant public attention due to its sensational nature. Many believed she was a witch or had supernatural powers, which added to her case's intrigue.

Her conviction was primarily based on the claims of the young family member. On December 8, 1885, Betsey Reed was hanged, making her the first woman executed in Illinois. The execution attracted a crowd of around 10,000 people, highlighting the macabre fascination with her story and the odd circumstances surrounding her death.

It wasn't long after her execution that stories began to spread about Betsey's ghost haunting Baker Cemetery, where she was buried next to her husband, Leonard. They share a newer tombstone, which features Leonard's name inscribed on the top with "Death by Murder" beneath it. Below, Betsey's name is listed, along with the inscription "Death by Hanging."

In the dead of night, whispers slither through the cold, moonlit graveyard, their voices barely audible, but unmistakably there. The air is thick, heavy with a palpable unease that clings to your skin like the damp chill of a tomb. As the shadows stretch unnaturally long, stretching toward you like fingers eager to clutch, the silence is broken only by the distant rustle of dead leaves.

It is here, in this forsaken place, that the White Lady is said to roam—her presence a chilling specter that sends shivers down the spine of anyone unlucky enough to cross her path. Her appearance is as unsettling as it is tragic—a pale, nearly translucent figure in a tattered gown, fluttering like wisps of fog. Her dress billows eerily around her, flowing and twisting as though alive with ghostly energy. She moves without sound, gliding between the tombstones as if weightless, her hollow eyes fixed forward, staring into eternity.

Her story is a tale drenched in sorrow and injustice. Bound to this graveyard by the weight of her wrongful conviction, the White Lady was a woman betrayed in life and sentenced to an agonizing death. Her cries, stifled by the cold, indifferent hands of fate, echo in the wind, lost to the world of living.

But even in death, she lingers, her spirit unwilling to rest until justice is served—a haunting reminder of the power of vengeance and betrayal.

Those who have dared to speak of her—those brave or foolish enough to venture into the graveyard at night—claim to have seen her drifting among the stones, her eyes wide with an unspoken agony, as if searching for something...or someone. Her gaze, cold and hollow, is said to pierce through the very soul, chilling to the core, making it clear that there is no escape from her unholy wrath.

And if you listen closely, the wind may carry her mournful wail—soft at first, like the rustling of dead leaves, then growing louder, anguished, as though calling out for the justice that was stolen from her. She is not a spirit that will simply fade with the dawn; she is bound to the graveyard, her sorrow turned to fury, forever seeking, forever waiting. Anyone who dares to approach her domain might find themselves frozen in place, lost in the unblinking stare of the White Lady, a soul forever lost in time, never to return.

For those who have looked into her eyes and felt her cold breath on their skin, there is no forgetting. The White Lady does not simply haunt the graveyard; she claims the souls of those who dare trespass, dragging them into the shadows with her, where they, too, will become part of her tragic tale—trapped in the eternal, restless night.

Indiana
Avon Haunted Bridge

In the heart of Avon, a large concrete train bridge stands tall above County Road 625 East, just south of Highway 36. Built in 1906, this impressive structure is both broad and commanding. Below the bridge, a busy road sees constant traffic rushing by. Those nearby hear haunting screams and moans when a train rushes overhead.

During the bridge's construction, a worker was cutting a wooden beam to size, as it was too long. He was standing on the wooden framework that supported the bridge. While he was sawing, cement was being poured into a support below.

Unfortunately, he lost his balance and fell into the freshly poured cement. Unable to reach the man in time, the cement dried with the saw sticking out along with part of his hand. Initially, visitors to the bridge noticed something protruding—a rusty saw with a corpse's hand gripping it. After some time, the hand rotted away, but the rusty saw remained, serving as a reminder of the poor man's fate sealed within the cement. Even now, when a train passes overhead, the weight presses down on the concrete, and the spirit of the man who became part of the bridge he helped build moans, groans, and screams.

Linda Degh collected another narrative about the bridge in an old book on Indiana folklore.

"Somewhere in southern Indiana when there was a big, modern bridge that was gonna be built. And this woman and her little boy went down to look at the bridge, you know, the construction of this bridge. And the little boy had a little sand pail with a little metal shovel in it. And he was walking along the side there, and he fell in, and there was some wet cement. And his little shovel got locked in this wet cement halfway down the water. And the little shovel's still there. And if you go there at night, and the moon's out, and you walk along where this bridge is, and look at that shovel, you can hear the mother screaming for her little boy—"

Iowa
Things that Go Bump in the Night

"From ghoulies and ghosties and long-leggedy beasties and things that go bump in the night, Good Lord deliver us." Unknown Author

Villisca, Iowa, was a typical sleepy, close-knit Midwestern community surrounded by farms in the summer of 1912. Most people went to bed at a reasonable hour and woke up early the next day to follow the same routine they always had. Not much changed over time, and there was a sense of comfort in that stability.

Modest wooden homes painted in soft pastels with white picket fences lined the streets, echoing the joyful voices of children playing in the yards before the heat of the midday. The sound of a tin water bucket occasionally clanged as it was set against the outside water pump. The pump handle emitted a squeaking noise as it was pushed up and down to draw water from the cistern or well. Little arms worked diligently, see-sawing the handle to help their parents with daybreak chores like fetching water for breakfast.

In the early morning, oil and gas lamps illuminated their homes, accompanied by the chirping of crickets, barking of dogs, and the occasional snort or whinny of horses outside. As the morning awakened the sleeping inside, birds chattered, and an occasional rooster crowed. At the same time, the ambiance was occasionally interrupted by the sounds of trains passing through nearby tracks. From open windows, muffled conversations from neighbors refreshed from a night's sleep and ready for their morning routines drifted on the breeze. The aroma of freshly blooming flowers, the pungent scent of a farmer cleaning manure from a barn outside of town, and the smell of freshly cut grass from a lawn mower mingled with the delightful fragrances of roasted chicken, biscuits, and apple pie baking, creating a comforting atmosphere. That was every morning in Villisca, Iowa, where only the night before, most of the community families were seen walking home from church services and Sunday school, their laughter and chatter filling the air.

But on June 10, 1912, tranquility was shattered as news spread of a gruesome discovery that disrupted the peaceful slumber of the town: a brutal massacre had taken place, enveloping those within in an eerie silence. It echoed with horrors and everything unknown and feared that seemed to go bump in the night.

It happened in a tiny white three-bedroom home on Second Street belonging to 43-year-old Josiah "Joe" Moore. The family had resided there for about nine years. The house featured a parlor, a downstairs sewing room, a kitchen, an outhouse, and an upstairs attic crawl space. There was no electricity or running water inside. Joe was married to 39-year-old Sara, and together, they had four children: Herman (11), Katherine (10), Arthur (7), and Paul (5). Joe was part of a large extended family, many of whom lived in Villisca, including his parents and six siblings. He was a prominent citizen who had left his job at the local hardware and agricultural store to work for another resident, Frank Jones, an Iowa State Senator. Joe opened his own implement and vehicle store across the street, J.B. Moore Implement Company, which included a John Deere dealership, creating significant competition for Jones.

On the late afternoon of June 9, 1912, after rehearsing for a special presentation at the local church, Sara and the children left around 4:00 p.m. to visit Joe's parents, as they typically did every Sunday. Afterward, they attended the evening program at the Presbyterian Church. Two friends of 10-year-old Katherine—8-year-old Ina May Stillinger and her 12-year-old sister Lena Gertrude—were invited to stay the night at the Moore's home as a special treat. Joe called the Stillinger home to get their permission to stay, as the girls were afraid to walk to their grandmother's house after dark. After the performance, the family and their two young friends arrived home at about 9:30 p.m. And that is all we know—for something very wicked was waiting for them within.

Was there one person or more? Did he hide in a crawl space or under the children's beds, creeping out with a smug, evil smile on his lips after the family fell asleep? Did a killer lurk by a window or in a dark corner of the room, watching the children being tucked into bed with gentle kisses on a cheek?

Did he creep out then on tiptoes with a smug, evil smile, his mouth salivating and his heart pounding as he awaited the event? Only the murderer knows what happened that night.

On June 10, 1912, eight people in the home were murdered with an axe sometime between midnight and 2:00 a.m. The crime scene was not discovered until the following morning when Joe failed to respond to his clerk. Concerned neighbors broke into the locked house and stumbled upon the horrific massacre. While there were no signs of struggle elsewhere in the home, in the sewing room, which had been converted into a bedroom for Katherine, the Stillinger girls were found dead together in a single twin bed. Katherine and her brothers were in one bedroom, while their parents were in another. They had been murdered, and then the killer had returned to beat the faces so savagely that there were marks on the ceiling and walls, and the faces were unidentifiable. The murderer concealed the victims with cloths and clothing, as well as covering the windows and mirrors. He left the axe in the downstairs bedroom. After cleansing his hands in a pail of water, he prepared a meal of beans and locked the door behind him when he left.

The unsolved Villisca Axe Murders left a trail of shattered lives and a lingering curse that forever tainted the house. Over the years, visitors have dared to spend the night, but they leave with something more than they bargained for.

A shadowy figure is often seen drifting through the rooms, just as the whistle of the 2 a.m. train echoes through town— its mournful sound haunting the air. In the parlor bedroom, where the Stillinger girls met their end, the eerie giggles of children playing with an invisible companion send shivers down spines.

Items vanish only to reappear in strange places, and ghostly footsteps reverberate through the darkened halls.

Something is always watching. The house doesn't just invite the living; it ensnares them, urging everyone to leave lights on and peek beneath their beds for the sinister things that wait in the dark. Because the dead are there even if the killer has gone.

Kansas
A Ghost Stalks a Bridge

On Monday, September 13, 1897, a young boy made a chilling discovery—a partially buried body of a woman, twisted and unnaturally positioned, on a sandbar beneath the decaying Carbondale Railroad Bridge over the Kaw River near Lawrenceburg. Her body was upside down, her arms and shoulders cruelly wedged into the sand, half-submerged in the cold, shallow water. Terrified, he raced to alert the authorities, and soon, an undertaker and a coroner arrived to retrieve the body.

The woman was known to many—Lizzie Madden, a local figure whose life ended in a manner that sent chills down the spines of all who knew her. She had been returning home to North Lawrence from her parent's house in Weaver, taking the 10:45 Santa Fe train. Once she disembarked, she faced the long, eerie walk across the old bridge in the dark, late-night hours, alone, her footsteps echoing in the silence.

When the undertaker cleared the dirt and debris from her body, it was startlingly apparent—there were no signs of injury or bruises, no visible wounds to explain her demise. The assumption was that Lizzie had slipped through a missing railroad tie and plummeted to her death in the river below. Yet, something didn't sit right. Not long before her death, Lizzie had been threatening to expose several owners of illegal drinking establishments. She was set to testify in court, and those men had made it abundantly clear that she would never live to see the courtroom. Lizzie had been frightened, confiding in others about her growing terror.

Because of the lingering suspicion surrounding her death, the coroner's jury launched a formal inquiry. After reviewing the evidence, they declared it an accident—"There was not the slightest clue to attach suspicion to anyone," they concluded. The official records from Eudora Cemetery would later read: Lizzie Madden, age unknown, black, drowning, as the cause of death, marked February 28, 1897.

But the story didn't end with her death. Whispers spread like wildfire about Lizzie's restless spirit, now roaming the very bridge where her life was snuffed out. Her ghost, they said, appeared to those unlucky enough to cross the bridge at night. Sometimes, she materialized, writhing in agony as if trapped in some endless torment. At other times, she seemed to struggle violently, as though reliving her final, desperate moments.

The apparitions were so frequent and horrifying that townspeople soon began to avoid the bridge altogether after dusk. One night, a man recounted his experience crossing the bridge: "I was walking along, feeling my way over the ties when—Lord have mercy—right in front of me there was an object. I do not know what it was, but it moved around. I distinctly saw a representation of the murder of Liz Madden. I cannot be mistaken."

Half a dozen others reported seeing the ghost that weekend, all in the same haunted area. Years have passed, but Lizzie Madden's vengeful spirit never left. The old railroad bridge may have been torn down, but her restless presence clings to the river, hovering just beyond sight, waiting.

If you dare to stand on the banks of the Kaw River on a moonless night, you might hear her soft, agonizing whispers carried by the wind. Her voice, a chilling plea for justice, slices through the darkness as if she's still searching—searching for the one who took her life so violently and the souls to punish for it. If she cannot find them, she will come for their kin. Some say that if you listen closely enough, her cold fingers will brush against your skin, pulling you into the river's depths to join her in eternal unrest.

Kentucky
Goat Man Bridge

Things are lurking in the dark that no one should ever see. However, we cannot control when evil entities appear or what they might do to us if we cannot outrun them. One such creature is in the Fisherville neighborhood of Louisville, Kentucky. It hides beneath a railroad trestle bridge that spans Pope Lick Creek and has a terrifying reputation, waiting in the shadows for its prey, which includes small animals, the occasional stray pet, and unsuspecting humans. When trains zoom past overhead, creating deafening noise, the creature launches attacks on those below. It appears briefly before vanishing again.

This gruesome being walks upright on cloven feet, has goat-like horns, and a grotesque body that resembles both a human and goat. It mimics voices, and if someone mistakenly meets its gaze, it has the power to hypnotize individuals, drawing them into dangerous areas near the trestle.

A witness named Denise recounted an experience from 1975 when she was fifteen. She shared her story with the Kentucky Bigfoot Research Organization about a night spent with friends beneath the train trestle near Pope Lick Creek, deep in the woods. During this encounter, she saw a large, dark figure run across their path, much bigger than any human. The figure moved quickly, leaving them feeling terrified and prompting them to leave immediately. "It was VERY fast and much bigger than us. It was definitely on two legs, and it resembled a shadowy figure," Denise related. The experience was so terrifying that the group left immediately.

In the late 1980s, encountering the Pope Lick Monster, also known as the Goat Man, became a rite of passage for many teens. Numerous reports surfaced of strange figures spotted near the trestle during late-night adventures. One particular account involved a couple who claimed that as they drove beneath the trestle, a horned figure suddenly jumped out and grabbed their car door handle. Others recounted experiences where something clawed at their car doors when it was still possible to drive under the trestle.

The origins of the Pope Lick Monster are shrouded in mystery. Some believe it was once a circus freak frequently beaten by its owner and finally escaped via a train car. Others suggest that in the early 1900s, a farmer living along the creek fell on hard times during a drought and made a pact with the devil. When the sacrifice of one of his goats went wrong, he was transformed into a goat-man, now seeking vengeance on those who pass beneath the trestle.

One thing is sure: those who climb onto the trestle have only one thing to fear, and it is not the Goat Man. They are searching for something that isn't there while he lies on the ground in the shadows below. However, trains still speed down those tracks, and many have died from falls after neglecting to research the lore surrounding the beast and foolishly attempting to traverse the rails.

Louisiana
The Singing Bones

A large family with 25 children lived in a bayou below New Orleans, all squeezed into a tiny, palmetto-roofed shack. Food was scarce, and the mother had to divide even the smallest bits of fish or meat among them. Many nights, the little ones went to bed crying because their bellies growled with hunger. This constant struggle made the wife sullen and angry, resulting in her often yelling at her husband for various reasons, even blaming him for minor things like smoking his pipe.

One winter was particularly harsh, and the father came home one night without a bit of food for the children. Standing outside the rickety house, he pondered how he would explain to his wife and kids that he had nothing to give them. Tears welled in his eyes as he imagined their sad faces. Despite his apprehension, he took the difficult steps to the door and prepared to push it open.

Just as he entered, however, a wonderful scent of cooking meat filled his nostrils, and he was greeted by his happy children. One of them grabbed his hand and pulled him inside, and to his surprise, his usually ill-tempered wife was smiling as she gestured toward the table. In the center, there was a feast of boneless meat piled high.

That night, the family enjoyed their best meal in years. Over the next three days, they indulged in the delicious meat. The man thought about asking his wife where she had obtained such a meal, but he ultimately decided it wasn't worth the risk of being yelled at or upsetting her mood.

He also noticed that his wife was not eating with them, and he began to worry that she might be ill. To satisfy his curiosity, he decided to comment during supper. "This meat is delicious," he said, taking a bite of an exceptionally tender and juicy piece. "But it must be expensive since it has no bones." She replied that she purchased it that way, explaining that it was lighter to carry without the bones.

"Ah, I see. How about you sit and eat with us tonight?" the husband asked the wife. "I haven't seen you eat in days."

"I eat before you come home," she replied, "so I can care for the children."

He felt satisfied with her answer, but as he looked around the table, he noticed that one of his favorite sons was missing. Not wanting to upset his wife, he kept his thoughts to himself.

However, two weeks passed, and two more of their children failed to greet him when he came home. Concerned, he asked his wife where the children were.

She shrugged and replied, "I took them to their auntie's house to visit. They will be back in a while."

But they did not return. Another week went by, and still, another child disappeared. Growing increasingly uneasy, the man stepped outside for a walk to clear his mind. Upon returning home, he pondered how to approach his wife about the situation. Something was clearly wrong. He sat heavily on the back porch step, lit his pipe, and thought awhile.

As he sat there, he heard a low humming noise nearby. At first, he thought it was a bird, then perhaps a mosquito. However, the sound grew louder the longer he listened. It was the sound of children singing, and it was coming from a rock near his foot. "Our mother kills us. Our father eats us. We have no coffins. We are not on holy ground—"

The man dropped to his knees and towed up the stone. Beneath it, he could see so many small children's bones! He gasped, realization flooding over him. Now, he understood where his children had gone and where his wife had acquired the tender meat. He went inside the house, took up an axe, and killed the woman. He would not listen to her protests that there were too many children anyway. Then he buried the children in a cemetery, and he never ate meat again.

Maine
The Witch's Curse

Colonel Jonathan Buck, once hailed as a hero in Bucksport, Maine, is now remembered not only for his legacy but for the curse that clings to his grave. Though celebrated for his role in the Revolution and as the town's founder, a dark tale shadows his final resting place—a story born from his own command.

A woman, condemned as a witch, was sentenced to die by burning at Buck's order. As flames licked at her skin, she cursed him, promising to mark him for eternity. He laughed in her face. But, when Colonel Buck died, his grave marker—once pristine—became a grim reminder of her vengeance.

A stain, shaped like a woman's leg and foot, marred the granite, no matter how many times it was cleaned or how hard they tried to scrub it away. The mark always returned.

And it isn't just the stain that unsettles. Visitors to the grave often report an overwhelming sense of dread. Some swear they've seen a shadowy figure near the monument—an apparition, pale and cold, drifting silently in the mist. The curse lingers, a chilling reminder of the justice once dealt and the vengeance that will never fade. The footstep on the stone is just the beginning, for some say the woman's spirit still stalks the grounds, seeking something... or someone else.

Maryland
Pig Woman

The Pig Woman is not just a ghost; she is a curse—a living nightmare that haunts Russell Road in Maryland. The air there is always heavy with unease. The stink of decaying flesh and the reek of pig manure permeates the area. The land itself seems to whisper warnings to anyone who dares to pass by. Long abandoned and covered in moss, the bridge that spans the road is known as Pig Woman Lane. Her nightmare lingers there, bound forever to the site of her suffering.

In the 19th century, the woman was a living, breathing soul, but that all changed when a fire ravaged her farmhouse.

It consumed everything in its path. The flames twisted and snarled, overwhelming the house bit by bit. She was trapped on the second floor, forced to watch as her home turned into a fiery tomb. The smoke clawed at her lungs, and the heat singed her hair. Desperate, she leaped from the window, thinking she could escape, but the fall shattered her body. Her flesh melted away like wax under a flame, her nose pressed piggy-like flat, and her bones cracked under the violent impact of the ground.

But death did not claim her.

Instead, it left her broken and disfigured beyond recognition. Her face, once beautiful, was now a horrific mask of blackened skin and raw, exposed tissue with fragments of charred bone showing near her cheeks and chin. Her eyes were hollow, mere pits of shadow. She was reborn in fire, but what rose from the ashes was not a woman—it was something else. She was something twisted, angry, and evil enough to slaughter local pigs, peel the fresh flesh from their scalps, and use their face like a mask to cover her mangled features.

Driven mad by the horror of her survival, she crawled from the smoldering ruins of her home, dragging herself into the surrounding woods. Her desperate, pig-like cries echoed from her shattered windpipe in the night, but no one came to help. She sought refuge beneath the dark bridge, cowering there in fear until the anger began to rise within her.

Now, she is nothing more than a spectral nightmare. This twisted, grotesque figure roams the woods surrounding the bridge, waiting and watching. Once a simple crossing, the bridge has become her lair—a place where the very air feels thick with malice, and she can wreak out her punishment on anyone who crosses her path.

Cars that stop on the bridge often stall suddenly, the engine sputtering and dying just as she approaches the front bumper.

Those trapped inside are at her mercy. Those who dare to step out of the car on Pig Woman Lane speak of unnatural, disturbing sounds. They are grunts, snorts, and oinks resembling a pig in distress, but the noise emanates from beneath the bridge, from the darkness that lurks there. "Piggy Lady, Piggy Lady!" some call out. Those who do will hear the distant crunching of bones—perhaps the sound of something dragging itself from the muck, or worse, something that crawls beneath the earth, just out of sight. "Piggy Lady, Piggy—" It is said that once you've heard the sounds, she knows you're there. And you will catch her rotting skin stink.

Some have seen her form—a nightmarish caricature of a woman, burned and scarred, with flesh hanging like melted wax, her face a grotesque mask of agony. Her eyes are pools of black madness, unblinking and hollow, her mouth twisted into a grin that could only come from something long lost to humanity. And her hands are claws now, bent and sharp, like twisted branches from a decayed tree, capable of scratching, tearing, and raking against the car with a ferocity that can only be described as primal.

There are dark tales and whispers of a curse that cling to those who disturb her. One story is about a teenager who was full of arrogance and mocked the Pig Woman in her lair. He laughed at her disfigured form and taunted her with cruel words, believing she was nothing more than a phantom from a forgotten fairytale. However, the Pig Woman did not take kindly to such defiance. In an instant, she struck—a force unseen, a curse far older than anything the teenager could comprehend.

The boy's body twisted, and he shrieked, his skin hardening into something that was neither flesh nor bone—but rather something unnatural, bound to the earth. By the next morning, he was gone, consumed by the land he had mocked.

All that remained was a twisted, gnarled tree standing by the roadside, its bark etched with dark, ancient symbols. Those who pass by still claim they can hear the whisper of his voice in the gentle wind. It is a desperate plea from a soul forever trapped, serving as a warning to all who dare to disturb her.

The Pig Woman's rage is boundless, and those who encounter her are never the same. Some vanish without a trace, others are left marked by her touch, and a rare few may manage to escape.

Massachusetts
Hoosac Tunnel: Bloody Pit of Ghosts

If there were ever a place deserving the name "Bloody Pit," it would be the Hoosac Tunnel. This dark passage became a grave for many men who labored tirelessly, enduring enormous hardships to create a tunnel that seemed to lead straight to hell rather than running through the Berkshire Mountains. The dangerous and arduous nature of the undertaking resulted in the loss of numerous lives during its construction. It consumed many good sound men through its dark and gaping mouth. It chewed them to pieces and spit them out of its mungy gullet as ghosts.

The path running through the Hoosac Mountain Range connects the towns of Florida on the eastern end and North Adams on the western end. This four-and-three-quarter-mile stretch, which is completely dark, is still in use by freight trains today. During its construction, from 1851 to 1875, over 190 workers lost their lives due to various accidents. Although drowning, fire, or falling down the 1000-foot tunnel shaft were all popular ways to die in the tunnel, explosions tended to be the most widespread.

When tunnel construction began in the early 1850s, workers used gunpowder to blast through the mountain, which was a slow and tedious process. However, by 1866, nitroglycerin emerged as a new and faster method for excavation. This substance was not only ten times more potent than black powder but also significantly more unstable, leading to numerous fatalities. Often, the workers who handled it lacked sufficient training and qualifications.

On March 20, 1865, Ringo Kelley, Ned Brinkman, and Billy Nash were working in the tunnel when Kelley, the so-called "explosive expert" among them, prematurely detonated a nitroglycerin charge before Brinkman and Nash could reach safety. As a result, both Brinkman and Nash were trapped and buried alive under tons of rock while Kelley fled the scene.

However, the man who caused the accident returned, either by his own means or through some ghostly method. While not the leading cause of death in Hoosac, being murdered by the ghosts of coworkers was still a significant problem. Not long after Brinkman and Nash were buried alive, Kelley vanished. A passerby found his corpse near the location where his coworkers were killed; he had been choked to death. Many of the miners and those in the community believed that Brinkman and Nash had returned from the grave to murder the man who killed them. It did not seem so unconceivable.

For years, cries of agony swept out from the tunnel. Workers reported hearing eerie wails, moans, and groans so frequently that in September 1868, a manager involved in the construction of the Hoosac Tunnel, named Mr. Dunn, reached out to Paul Travers, a former cavalry officer and mechanical engineer. Dunn sought Travers's help researching and addressing his workers' concerns, who claimed to hear a man's voice crying out in agony within the tunnel. Paul Travers wrote to his sister on September 8, 1868: "Last night Mister Dunn and I entered the great tunnel (unfinished) at 9 p.m. We traveled about two miles into the shaft and then stopped to listen. As we stood there in the cold silence, we both heard what truly sounded like a man groaning out in pain. As you know, I have heard that sound many times during the war. Yet when we turned the wicks up on our lamps, no other human beings were in the shaft. I haven't been this frightened since Shiloh. Mister Dunn agreed that it wasn't the wind we heard. Perhaps Nash or Brinkman? I wonder."

Those who had worked with Nash and Brinkman shared the same story for several years. However, on June 15, 1872, at 11:30 p.m., Doctor Clifford J. Owens of Detroit had a far more terrifying experience. He entered the tunnel with James McKinstrey, a drilling operations superintendent, in order to investigate reports of strange sounds and ghostly apparitions troubling workers at the site.

As they ventured about two miles into the dark and cold tunnel, they stopped to take a break. Suddenly, they heard a mournful sound resembling someone in great pain. This eerie noise prompted them to look around, but they found no one else present besides themselves. In a letter, Owens later recounted the experience: "We had traveled about two miles into the shaft and were about to turn back when suddenly I heard a mournful sound."

Shortly afterward, Owens noticed a faint light coming from the west end of the tunnel. At first, he thought it was a workman carrying a lantern. However, as the light got closer, he realized it had an unusual blue hue. He seemed to transform into a headless figure floating above the ground. "It took the shape of a headless man," he wrote. "It came so close I could have touched it and it paused in front of us as if looking us over, then floated off toward the east end of the shaft and vanished into thin air." Doctor Owens considered himself a realist and typically avoided superstitions or fanciful stories. However, he later recounted the experience with such conviction that he couldn't dismiss what he and McKinstrey had witnessed right before their eyes.

A significant disaster occurred on October 17, 1868, when a gas explosion killed thirteen miners. While their bodies were missing, local residents reported seeing ghostly figures resembling miners carrying tools near the site. Once all the bodies were recovered and properly buried, these sightings reportedly stopped. However, strange noises continued to emanate from the tunnel.

One of the most notable accounts of ghostly signs comes from Joseph Impoco, a farmer and former railroad employee who worked in the Hoosac Tunnel in his younger years. Impoco reported several instances where he believed disembodied voices saved him during dangerous situations. While working on the tracks and "crouching alone in the tunnel's black wastes," as he described it, Impoco heard a voice urgently calling out to him: "Run, Joe! Run!" He stated, "I turned, and sure enough, there was No. 60 coming at me. Boy, did I jump back fast! When I looked, there was no one there."

The warning allowed him to leap out of harm's way before being struck by the speedy train. "I had seen a guy with a torch walk by, and he'd waved to me but hadn't paid any attention.

If that voice hadn't called to me, I would have been killed." He was confident that no one else was around when he heard this voice and could find no source.

A second time, Impoco was using a heavy iron crowbar to free some freight cars stuck on icy tracks. He once again heard the familiar voice shout, "Joe! Joe! Drop it, Joe!" He instinctively released the bar just as it struck an overhead, short-circuited power line carrying 11,000 volts of electricity. The force from the electrical surge would have caused serious injury had he not dropped the bar when he did. "Something made my hands open," Impoco divulged, "and the bar dropped."

Impoco reported a third warning while clearing trees when the familiar voice urged him, "Run, Joe, run!" He took off like lightning but tripped and fell, getting quite a bang from the tree. However, he stepped away unharmed. The crew laughed at his antics but noted another strange, almost otherworldly laugh joining in. When the crew suddenly clamped mouths shut, aware another voice was chiming in, the peculiar laugh continued, startling them all. One by one, the men in that crew, including Impoco, left their jobs at the tunnel for other work. Many cited the ghostly activity as the reason they left.

The unsettling stories of the Hoosac Tunnel are steeped in tragedy, marked by the lives lost during its brutal construction. In the suffocating darkness of the tunnel, shadows seem to flicker, and an eerie silence falls heavily in the air. Joseph Impoco's experiences suggest something not so malevolent lurked just out of sight as if the spirits of those who perished were watching from the depths to help him. Not everyone had that same experience. Most were left with a sense of anxiety and fear.

Whispers echo eerily through the Hoosac Tunnel, curling through the damp air like the last breath of the forgotten dead.

They carry warnings, unintelligible yet heavy with dread—a reminder that the past here is never truly buried.

As night falls and the entrance is swallowed by shadow, an uneasy stillness settles. The ground itself seems to breathe, and the tunnel—more wound than passage—feels less like a manmade structure and more like a living thing. Something ancient and angry stirs within.

Though trains still thunder through its depths, the tunnel is officially closed to trespassers. But that has never stopped the curious from staring into its entrance. Some claim to have heard the soft cadence of pickaxes in the distance, or the muffled groans of men crushed beneath rock.

Some who peer into the gaping mouth of the tunnel are never the same—eyes hollow, dreams plagued by the feeling of being watched by something just beyond the flicker of light. Something waiting in the dark. Something that never left.

And so the Hoosac Tunnel stands, not just a relic of engineering—but a mausoleum. A place that does not forget. And does not forgive.

Michigan
The Monster Lurks

Dark creatures walk among us, appearing human but driven by insidious, dark demons within. How often do we greet someone while passing them on the street or sitting next to them in church, our elbows touching and our eyes meeting from across the room as the preacher speaks about what we should avoid—things these hidden fiendish characters do? I would presume it is pretty often. Those most sinful excel at concealing their true nature, stifling true and wicked intentions behind a mask of compassion. They smile with playful eyes, but hidden beneath the smile is a haughty leer.

Their laughter is like a childish giggle, but it conceals a repressed sinister laugh. Unlike the little wild things like owls, tiny weasels, and coyotes who harmlessly hunt to survive, these entities search for their prey for pleasure, devouring them like a joy hunter seeks out his prey to shoot it for entertainment.

I speak of this because I am acquainted with this type of entity, this monster lurking. However, I have identified mine. Others are not so lucky. One family in Michigan would suffer due to their inability to see the hidden wickedness in someone and would ultimately pay the price. Here is their story—

One of the most chilling thoughts is that something sinister may be approaching us in the dark of night when we are at our most vulnerable—sleeping serenely. In the early hours of November 22, 1883, those inside the humble home of 74-year-old Jacob Crouch, located a few miles from Jackson, Michigan, slept peacefully to the gentle rumble of thunder, the gusts of wind against the walls, and the soft patter of rain on the roof. While the storms rolled through Spring Harbor Township, the sounds lulled them to sleep and masked the gunfire that erupted within the home just a few hours later.

Jacob Crouch, a prominent cattle farmer and wealthy landowner known for his frugality, was shot dead in his bed along with three others at around 3:00 a.m. Jacob suffered a gunshot wound to the head. His 33-year-old daughter, Eunice, who was eight months pregnant, sustained multiple wounds, including shots to her neck and head. Eunice's husband, 30-year-old Henry, was shot in the neck and abdomen. Moses Polley, a 26-year-old Pennsylvania cattle buyer and family friend who often traveled to Michigan for business with Jacob, had large amounts of cash on him and had stayed the night. He was shot behind the ear and in the chest.

Although robbery, inheritance disputes, and family conflicts were believed to have contributed to the slayings, no murderer was ever brought to justice. A 16-year-old hired hand named George Bolles, who slept in the upstairs room, awoke to the sounds of gunshots, thumping, and a groan that resembled someone saying, "Oh—oh!" Fearing for his life, he hid in a trunk at the foot of his bed until the early hours of the morning. When he finally emerged, he discovered the body of Jacob and rushed to the neighbor's house in panic.

Another servant, 33-year-old Julia, who slept near the pantry, was unaware of the events unfolding around her. She remained oblivious, continuing her morning breakfast routine until a neighbor stopped by. As word spread throughout the nearby farms and community, chaos ensued, with curious onlookers entering the home. By the time the sheriff finally arrived at the murder scene, much of the evidence had been trampled and compromised.

Initial suspects in the case included George Bolles, the farmhand who discovered the bodies; Julia Reese, the housekeeper; and family members Judd Crouch, Jacob's son (who was raised by his eldest daughter, Susan, and believed she was his mother until he was ten years old); Daniel Holcomb, Jacob's eldest daughter's husband; and Byron Crouch, Jacob's son. Speculation also pointed to other rivals, business associates, and family over inheritance disputes. Ultimately, despite numerous investigations and trials, no one was ever convicted of these heinous crimes, leaving the shadow of the dark figure still looming. Tragically, it seemed he was not done, as suspicious deaths continued. On January 2, 1884, Jacob Crouch's daughter Susan was found dead in her bed. Reports about her cause of death conflicted. Some suggested she was poisoned, while others claimed she died from natural causes due to heart failure.

Farmhand James Foy, who worked for the Holcombs, was found shot in the head just two days after Susan's death. Foy was known to speak openly about the Crouch murders in local pubs, leading some to believe he might have been silenced because he knew too much about the case. His death was ruled a suicide. A neighbor reportedly went insane and died in agony, which fueled local rumors about supernatural influences or curses linked to the murders. Additionally, another man from Jackson became convinced that he was responsible for the family's deaths and ultimately committed suicide, which deepened the sense of tragedy and reinforced the belief in a possible curse associated with this case.

Detective Galen Brown, assigned to the Crouch case, was walking back from the Crouch farmhouse on the road to Horton when a buggy with two men pulled up beside him. After asking his name, they shot him. Brown survived the attack and identified Judd Crouch as one of the two men who fired the shots. Eventually, the Crouch house burned down.

However, strange events followed. In the aftermath of this gruesome crime, many people turned to spiritualism, and séances became a way for them to attempt to communicate with the deceased victims in hopes of uncovering the truth about their deaths or providing them with peace.

In January 1885, the Grand Rapids Morning Telegram reported that a medium claimed to have spoken with Jacob Crouch. According to the medium, Jacob stated that none of his family members were responsible for the murders. Instead, he identified a relative of George Bolles, the 16-year-old farmhand who worked for Jacob Crouch, as the real culprit. This individual had initially intended only to rob Jacob, whom the thief believed had considerable money. He gave the boy some chloral to mix into the cider, but the amount was insufficient to achieve the desired effect.

When he approached Jacob's bed, Jacob awoke, prompting the intruder to shoot him. The noise startled Eunice White, whom he first struck senselessly to the floor. Fearing that others might wake up before he could escape with his loot, he shot them as well, including Mrs. White, whom he then placed back in bed. The medium also suggested that Foy's suicide was the result of a drunken spree, stemming from his fear of being arrested for the murders.

Shortly after the brutal murders, chilling whispers began to spread—tales of a ghostly figure seen drifting between St. John's Cemetery, where Eunice was laid to rest, and Reynolds Cemetery, where her father Jacob's grave lies in quiet decay. Witnesses described a pale, formless mist gliding silently along the path, pausing only at Jacob's stone before dissolving into the night air, as if still waiting for something... or someone.

The terrifying sightings gave rise to an annual vigil held on November 21, the anniversary of the bloodshed. Locals gather in hushed fear, clutching candles, eyes fixed on the shadows—hoping to glimpse the spirit and praying it does not see them.

But the most dreadful part of the tale lies not in the ghostly mist but in the man who walked away. The murderer was never found. He lived among the unsuspecting for years—smiling at neighbors, chatting with strangers, brushing shoulders in the market. Perhaps he fathered others. Perhaps one of them is watching you now. Maybe they walk your street, step onto your porch, and place a hand on your doorknob...

Did you remember to turn the locks tonight?

Minnesota
The Wendigo

The Cree people have a significant presence in Canada and historically in Minnesota, with their accounts of the Wendigo long passed down in the state. In Cree mythology, the Wendigo is depicted as a malevolent spirit that can inhabit a human host. This possession often occurs when an individual is consumed by negative traits such as greed and gluttony. Still, it can also happen due to extreme hunger. The Wendigo is believed to enter a person through biting or manifesting in dreams. Once possessed, the individual may exhibit violent and erratic behavior, often leading to cannibalism as they turn against those around them.

If you think this could never happen, look at your family and friends. At what point would each of them become so desperate that they would be willing to kill for something they want or need?

Before you answer, consider that you have never witnessed a single stale cracker sitting on a table for a week while eight people starve, unable to access a grocery store for food. Who would be the first to give in to despair and imagine, with a pinch of salt, pepper, and herbs, that your forearm or calf could be a tender, flavorful, juicy, and perfectly cooked meal? People have been murdered for far less.

In 2018, a 16-year-old strangled to death his 20-year-old sister over a dispute regarding the household Wi-Fi password. On May 10, 1982, three employees at a restaurant in Mount Pleasant, Texas, were brutally shot and bludgeoned during a robbery that yielded just $100. An obsession with a condiment spiraled into deadly violence in April 2022 when Glenn Hirsch received a scanty amount of duck sauce for his order. He followed the delivery driver and shot him dead.

Swift Runner was a Plains Cree trapper in Canada in the late 1870s who had a happy life, complete with a wife and children. However, during one particularly severe winter, his family faced starvation. After the death of his eldest son, Swift Runner resorted to cannibalism despite being close to a Hudson's Bay Company post where they could have obtained food and supplies. Over the winter, the trapper killed, dismembered, and consumed his wife and five remaining children, overwhelmed by hunger and the need to eat human flesh. Upon his return to the camp after winter, he acted oddly. When confronted, he confessed to being possessed by a Wendigo. For your information, Swift Runner was hanged for his crime.

Wendigos are usually simple to identify in human form.

They become so famished that they eat their own lips down to the nub and appear as if they are baring their teeth. Once a human becomes sick, is believed to be a Wendigo, and has tasted human flesh, nothing can save them. In the late 1890s, a couple of women from Whitefish Lake were brought in for treatment after one of them dreamed that her deceased brother offered her a tender, savory piece of human flesh delicately spread out in a bowl of ice. The women fell seriously ill and were believed to be Wendigos; however, since they did not consume human flesh, both eventually recovered.

Big Trout Lake is in Canada, north of Minnesota, and home to the Cree community. A woman and her husband traveled from Wapiska, 80 miles away, to visit the husband's father at Big Trout Lake in January 1896. The husband, Na-pa-nin, was 35 years old and well-liked in his community. He was a good father and seemed healthy as they started their journey to Trout Lake. However, on the second night of their travels, he began to act strangely, distrustfully, and suspiciously, claiming that animals were trying to attack him. His condition continued to deteriorate throughout the journey until his paranoia left him staring a bit uncomfortably and hungrily at his wife and children. Eventually, the wife urged him to go ahead of the family to his father's, fearing for their safety. By the time they reached Big Trout Lake, his mental state had severely declined. His fits and violent episodes worsened over the nearly three weeks they spent at his father's home. His body began to swell, his belly bloated, and his lips were almost chewed off. During their journey home to Wapiska, the man's hostile behavior escalated significantly. He threatened those close to him, shouting that if they were so distressed about his violent and aggressive behavior, they should kill him.

Fearing for their safety, members of the community bound the man's hands and feet while his wife left with their baby.

The men discussed the possibility of killing him but had yet to reach a decision. However, when he broke free from his bindings in a state of frantic delirium, they feared he would harm them all. Knowing that an axe must be used instead of a gun to kill a Wendigo, they struck him four times in the head. His fate was sealed at that moment. His body was burned, and trees were felled over the grave. Many days passed before the community began to fear that he might reappear, but he never did.

Once more, I pose the question: at what moment will each of your friends or family members reach such a level of desperation to survive that they could consider taking a life for something they want, desire, or need? The next time you catch any of them nervously nibbling on their lips or casting curious glances your way as if you're a succulent morsel, take a moment to reflect on their plight. Observe the hunger in their eyes, a mix of fear and longing, suggesting that their need for sustenance may push them to extreme measures. Remember that survival can transform even the gentlest individuals into something unrecognizable when faced with dire circumstances. They are always one step away from becoming that Wendigo, and you are their next meal.

Mississippi
Goat-man of Devil Worshipper Road

Waynesboro Shubuta Road—known by locals in hushed tones as Devil Worshipper Road—is a stretch of Mississippi Highway 510 that cuts through the dense, brooding woods of northern Wayne County and southern Clarke County. Though officially a state highway, the road is more infamously remembered for what prowls its shoulder after dark.

According to grim local lore, this lonely stretch once served as a meeting ground for a hidden satanic cult. Beneath the veil of southern moonlight, the cult gathered among the pines, whispering in dead languages, offering bloody sacrifices.

They used goats, dogs, even children, some say—in exchange for power beyond understanding. And at the black heart of it all was a desperate farmer, ruined by drought and madness, who struck a bargain no man should ever make. He traded his soul for wealth—and became the Goat-man.

Twisted by his own sin, the man's body grotesquely transformed. Standing nearly seven feet tall, this hulking creature lurches along the roadside at night—half-man, half-beast, with muscular, fur-covered legs, curling horns, and eyes that burn like dying coals. He is said to carry a rusted pitchfork—perhaps once a farmer's tool, now a cursed weapon—and to stalk any who wander too close to the woods.

Drivers report heart-stopping glimpses of the Goat-man just beyond their high beams—only to blink and find him gone. Then come the hoof prints... stamped across the hoods of cars, as though he had leaned close, breathing against the glass, deciding.

But the most terrifying stories are reserved for those who didn't leave fast enough. Tales of engines stalling with no explanation...of hands trembling on the ignition as something shifts in the back seat. And when the brave dare to look in the rearview mirror, they see him—his massive shape looming silently, his burning eyes fixed on theirs.

He never speaks. He doesn't have to.

The Goat-man waits for the greedy, the reckless, the curious—and once you see him, it may already be too late. The legend warns: if you hear hooves behind you on Devil Worshipper Road, don't stop. Don't look back. And for God's sake... don't blink.

Missouri
Headless Cobbler of Smallett Cave

Hidden deep in the remote wilds of southwest Missouri, near the ghostly remnants of a place once called Smallett, lies a cave swallowed by time and forest. Barely marked on any map, it sits off an old road on private land, untouched by modern life—and for good reason. For over 150 years, no one has dared linger near its dark mouth after sunset. It is said to have a haunt, or "haint," as it is called in some regions. The cave's haunting dates back to the blood-soaked days of the Civil War. George Evans, a humble cobbler and quiet Union sympathizer, was a hunted man. Confederate Guard soldiers in the region were ruthless, killing foes indiscriminately.

Evans, desperate to avoid their wrath, retreated to the cave—his hammer striking leather deep within its hollow. By night, he crept silently home, shrouded by shadows.

But one night, the shadows betrayed him.

A group of Confederate raiders caught him just outside the cave while he was *tap-tap-tap* tapping on a boot. They said nothing. They didn't need to. They just murdered him and cut off his head. Evans' severed noggin was never found.

Since then, the cave has never known peace.

Locals speak in whispers of a strange red light, like a lantern burning hellfire, gliding silently above the treetops, drawn to intruders. Some claim the light follows them all the way home, hovering just beyond their windows until dawn. An icy tap-tap-tapping echoes endlessly inside the cave—unnatural and steady, like a hammer pounding hide from the other side of death.

But it's what roams outside that freezes the blood. At dusk, on certain nights, a headless figure lurches down the old road and through the trees—its balance unnatural, its movement jerky, like a marionette controlled by cruel, unseen hands. Slung around its neck is a gruesome clump of shoes, the soles slapping against its chest with each dragging step. The red lights drift with it—silent sentinels glowing between the trees. They say if you hear the *tap-tap-tap* tapping, it's already too late. And if the lights appear, don't run. He can smell fear... even without a head.

Many accounts come from residents like the Sellar family, who have lived on the property since the late 1800s. In Ozark's Live, a cultural preservation project documenting the region's people and places, Steven Sellers recounted, "They would see a red light going up the creek bed. They couldn't hear anything, but they could see a light down there. A red light of some sort, and it would move."

In the late Walter Darrell Haden's book, "The Headless Cobbler of Smallett Cave," he recounts a story from his grandmother, Frances Kay Haden Moten. One night, her mother and another woman were walking along an old path by Spring Creek and the cave to keep watch with a woman who was dying of consumption. Missus Moten shared this account: "Ma told us later that just about 'dusky dark' a man without a head stepped out into the road in front of them," she related. "On one of his shoulders he had a Bible. As the two women and the headless man met, he didn't say a thing, Ma said, but the women lit out, and the strange man walked on in the opposite direction. They hurried on east to the Cloud home, where later that night the sick woman died. Mrs. Hall, Ma, and her sister, Aunt Julia Sellers, laid out the corpse for burial while the menfolks started work on a casket. It was a hot night, so the womenfolks, when their work was done, sat down in some cane-bottom chairs to cool awhile in the yard of the home. Ma had leaned back in her chair while she smoked her clay pipe. All of a sudden from between the back of her chair and the side of an old earthen cellar, a commotion began. At first, she thought that it was the headless haint. I reckon for awhile there was almost another woman to be laid out. But then she found out it was just her chair mashing a calf that had been dozing alongside the cellar. The calf lit out, and so did Ma."

So, if you ever find yourself near Smallett, Missouri—if your car stalls on that lonely road or a wrong turn draws you too close to the cave's forgotten mouth—heed the sounds around you—whether loud or soft. It may not be a calf making a ruckus in the field nearby. It just might be something more gruesome—that headless haint.

Listen closely for the *tap-tap-tap* of the old hammer to leather. Watch the tree line. And whatever you do, don't follow the lights.

They say the Headless Cobbler still wanders, seeking the hands that took his life... or perhaps a new head to make his own so he can make things right. And should you hear the slow, rhythmic *tap-tap-tap* of a hammer on leather in the dead of night—pray it stays distant.

Because once it stops...the cobbler's right behind you.

Montana
Bannack's Dead Return

Bannack, Montana, was founded in 1862 by gold-hungry miners from Colorado who struck fortune in the shimmering veins of Grasshopper Creek. The town flourished in its early years, bustling with dreams and desperation. But as the gold thinned and shadows thickened, Bannack began to die—slowly, almost as if the earth itself were reclaiming what had been taken. By the 1970s, the last stubborn souls drifted away, leaving behind empty buildings, hollow echoes, and something else...

Today, Bannack stands frozen in time within the borders of Bannack State Park. Some say its silence is misleading because nothing truly leaves a town like this. Well, at least not some of its residents—those whose souls are stuck in this ghost town because they lived and died here.

Henry Plummer served as the sheriff of Bannack, elected in 1863. He also led a gang of outlaws known as the "Innocents." On January 10, 1864, he was hanged by vigilantes due to accusations of robbery and murder that had terrorized the mining community. Since his death, his ghost has been reported in various locations around Bannack, especially near the Skinner Saloon and Chrismans' Store.

However, during its period as a mining community, his ghostly tale was overshadowed by a tragic incident that occurred in August 1916. Sixteen-year-old Dorothy Dunn went to Grasshopper Creek on the outskirts of town with her friend Ruth Wornick and her cousin Fern Dunn to wade and swim. While playing, the girls accidentally stepped over a steep ledge and fell into deep water, but none of them could swim. A 12-year-old boy was able to rescue Ruth and Fern, but tragically, Dorothy drowned. Her body was recovered several hours later.

Shortly after the tragic drowning, Dorothy's friend, Bertie Matthews—whose parents ran the Meade Hotel—was the first to speak of seeing a ghost. She swore Dorothy appeared to her one evening, soaked and shivering, wearing a pale blue dress clinging to her ghostly form. Her eyes were empty. Her mouth never moved, but Bertie said she heard her speak.

Since then, visitors to the old hotel, now swallowed by the ghost town of Bannack State Park, have claimed to see a girl in a blue dress staring silently from an upstairs window—just before she fades into nothing. Some say they hear the soft dribble of water on hardwood, even when the floors are dry.

They catch a whiff of mungy lake wafting in the air. And hear the distinct sound of gurgling, like someone whose throat is filled with liquid. Others swear the window fogs from the inside as if someone... or something... is still watching.

Nebraska
Hanged Man's Bridge

In 1907, Pender, Rosalie, and Bancroft communities were small agricultural towns near the Iowa border in Thurston County, Nebraska. Many families in these towns were involved in farming. Among them were Walter "Bud" Copple and his wife, Eva, who were both 36 years old. They had seven children, ranging from their youngest twins, who were just two months old, to their eldest, 13-year-old Blanche. They employed a hired hand, Fred Burke, to assist with their farm. He was clean-shaven, boyish, standing five feet nine inches tall, and 29 years old. They were unaware that their farmhand's actual name was Loris Higgins, not the name he had previously given them.

But there was a lot they did not know about the man which would later come back to haunt them. Burke had a troubled past marked by alcohol abuse and violent behavior. If they had known this, perhaps the horrific actions he would commit against the Copple family would never have occurred. But at 2 a.m. on May 13, 1907, Burke, who was heavily intoxicated and had been increasingly angry over the past few weeks due to what he perceived as "an overwhelming workload," went outside to smoke a cigarette.

Shortly afterward, Walter Copple stepped outside to check on some young pigs and a horse he had been concerned about. At that moment, Burke took a gun and beat Copple with the stock, then shot him in the belly and the head. The eldest daughter, Blanche, ran to the door after hearing her father's cries and tried to get outside, but Burke stopped her with his hand, telling her that thieves were trying to break into the house. "You get into the house, damn you," he lashed out, "and put out the light, see that you stay there; there are burglars out there, and they'll all kill you if you go out." Then he ran to get more ammunition.

When Eva heard the commotion and ran outside to check on her husband, Burke also clubbed her with a 27-inch hickory baseball bat, one of the children's toys, and then shot her in the head with the gun. The bat was later found covered in blood and hair. The weapon was subsequently discovered in a haystack, with unspent shells still inside and the stock split.

The corpses were dragged to the hog pens and hurled inside. Burke then went inside the home and made himself comfortable while the curious children began to rouse. The eldest daughter, Blanche, age 13, told authorities that after killing her parents, Burke came into the house and told the children to go back to bed. His eyes were bulging in their sockets, and his hair was askew, his clothes covered in blood.

He quickly locked the doors and windows and blew out the lamps so she could not see the bodies or long trails of blood. But she knew something was amiss. "Why don't Mamma and Papa come and care for the children?" she asked of Burke.

He shrewdly answered, "They're out in the hog pen watching for the burglars."

"I don't believe it." she hissed. "You have killed Papa and Mamma. I know it because they would not leave us here alone like this." Burke tried to make the children believe their parents were safe, and then Blanche asked Burke to light a lamp because the 2-month-old twins were crying.

"Let the little brats cry," Burke had spat at her. "I won't light a lamp." Blanche stayed awake in the dark, taking care of the children. Later, she would relate, "Every time the old hen in the entryway would cackle, he would jump up and point his gun out the window." Before dawn, Burke left, stealing the family's mule.

Then, in the morning, 7-year-old Tommy ventured into the yard to begin his chores and found his parents' bodies being eaten by the hogs.

"I had to fight the hogs for a long time," the child told authorities, "To keep them away from Papa and Mamma."

Ten-year-old Sumner ran to the neighbors, who notified local authorities, and Burke was quickly apprehended while drinking heavily at a saloon. "I don't know why I did it. I don't remember hearing Copple leave the house," Burke would confess to them. "I was sick and went out and vomited. I saw him coming back from the barn. I just got the gun and shot him. I didn't look for any money and was not after any. I did not have over 2 dollars at any time after the shooting."

Burke was held at the county jail in Omaha due to concerns about a mob seeking justice, dragging him out for a lynching.

Recently, too many criminals had been dodging accountability by claiming insanity and then escaping the asylums holding them. Their failure to take responsibility demonstrated a lack of concern for the innocent lives impacted by their actions. The family was much beloved, and they wanted to avenge the deaths and ensure it did not happen again.

So, when the train hauling Burke stopped near Bancroft while transporting him back to Pender for his trial for the double murder, a mob of 20 to 30 masked men emerged from the shadows. They disconnected the train and overpowered the officers escorting the killer. They loaded him into a wagon and moved along the streets.

Five-year-old Frank Copple, one of the sons of the murdered couple, was playing nearby when the strange procession rushed past. Curiously, he called out for his aunt, not initially noticing Burke among them. Once he spotted the murderer standing there, he became frightened and began to cry uncontrollably. He pointed a stubby finger at Burke and shouted, "Oh, there's Burke! He's coming after me!" Terrified, he bolted into the house.

The boy didn't realize that his worries would soon be relieved at the nearby Logan Bridge. Burke was dragged off the wagon with his feet shackled and a rope tightly secured around his neck. Between 9 and 10 a.m. on August 26, 1907, Burke dropped seven feet from the bridge with a crackle and pop of neck and vertebrae and began to swing, his neck awkwardly tilted. His head dangling like a floppy doll from a two-year-old's chubby hand. Those of the mob riddled his body with bullets and then dispersed.

A passenger named Cummins, on the same train as the slain man, had crept through a field. He concealed himself wisely in the crops and stayed hidden to watch the spectacle.

"While I don't believe in mob law," said Mr. Cummins, "that fellow got what he deserved. I thought I'd see that fellow hanged." Burke's flannel shirt and hanging rope were cut into pieces and issued as souvenirs. His body was sent to Denver, Colorado. However, his despicable soul remains trapped between Bancroft and Pender, particularly at the old bridge. For years, locals and travelers of the Omaha Reservation have refused to go near the old bridge due to the presence of his ghost.

He floats upward from the depths where he was dangling from the bridge, his form rising slowly and unnaturally. With each inch gained, a chilling silence envelops the air, broken only by the muted gush of water beneath the bridge. It is followed by a crackling and popping sound, the same exploding echoes that broke the air when the rope connected to the noose was pulled straight and tight with his weight, and his neck and spine were stretched apart.

He finally settles on the cold, damp surface of the bridge, his presence unsettling and bizarre. His hands are folded over his legs, his head hangs awkwardly against his chest, and his neck is elongated like a turkey's neck before it makes its last gobble on Thanksgiving Day. *Phhhh-guhhhh* is the sound of air struggling to work through his windpipe and the twisted remnants of his neck. *Phhhh-guhhhh.* Shadows twist around him as if they are alive, reaching out to embrace his ghostly figure. *Phhhh-guhhhh.* His eyes gleam with an otherworldly light, reflecting a darkness that seeps into souls, enticing them to join him in more killing sprees because Burke isn't quite finished yet. *Phhhh-guhhhh.* Because he does not realize he is dead.

Nevada
The Dead Don't Sleep

Julie Bulette arrived in Virginia City in 1859, drifting in with the winter winds like a bad omen. The town was young, greedy, and rabid—fattened by the discovery of the Comstock Lode, its veins coursing with silver and sin. Beneath the glittering promise of wealth, Virginia City was rotting. Saloons overflowed with violence, gambling halls reeked of desperation, and the red-light district pulsed like a wound that would never close. Julie, one of the few women among thousands of hardened, dust-covered men, was beautiful in a way that stirred something primal.

They said her smile could silence a room, and her eyes held secrets that made strong men shudder. But beauty like that doesn't stay untouched for long. She made her living pleasing those whose souls had long since blackened. Every night, the flicker of lamplight in her cottage window marked another transaction, another inch closer to something monstrous.

On the morning of January 20, 1867, silence hung over her cottage like a shroud. When they found her, the horror was unspeakable—strangled, her skull bashed in, her body left as if the killer wanted the town to see. To feel what had been done. It wasn't just a murder—it was a message, though no one dared decipher it.

The town demanded blood. Within a year, they had their scapegoat: John Millain, a drifter with a foreign accent and haunted eyes. He swore he hadn't killed her, only helped loot the place after her death. But truth had no place in the gallows' shadows. They hanged him as the townspeople jeered—yet as his neck snapped, the wind screamed through the streets like something ancient had been disturbed.

That's when the sightings began. People spoke of a woman in a tattered velvet gown, her face pale and luminous, her throat mottled with phantom bruises. She appears in windows long boarded up, walks hallways that no longer exist, and wails through the canyon winds on cold, moonless nights. Lights flicker. Doors burst open.

They say her soul was torn violently from her body, and now it stains the land like blood that won't wash out. And some swear—on dark, breathless nights—they've seen her shadow hover over men's beds, pressing down, whispering ancient curses in a voice like rust and smoke. Julie Bulette was murdered. For that, she is furious. And in Virginia City, where silver runs like blood and the earth remembers every scream, the dead don't sleep. They get revenge.

New Hampshire
Ghosts and Ghouls and Dead Girls on Smuttynose Island

The Isles of Shoals are a group of small islands and tidal ledges located about six miles off the east coast of the United States, straddling the border between Maine and New Hampshire. This area consists of nine islands known for their sparse vegetation and rocky terrain. Over the years, the islands have served various purposes, including seasonal fishing camps, summer resorts, and private homes.

Among these islands is the tiny 25-acre Smuttynose Island, named by local fishermen who thought the abundant seaweed at one end resembled the "smutty nose" of a large sea creature. The island is infamous for a gruesome murder that took place within its glooms, forever linked to the restless spirits said to roam its shores.

In the early 1870s, Norwegian fisherman John Hontvet and his wife, Maren, were the only residents of the isolated Smuttynose Island. John owned a schooner named the Clara Bella and rented a two-story duplex known locally as "The Red House." After some time, John's brother, Matthew, came to the island to fish with him. Maren's sister, Karen, also joined them initially but later moved to a nearby island to work at a hotel, visiting only occasionally thereafter.

During this time, the couple welcomed a destitute German fisherman, 28-year-old Louis Wagner, into their home, providing him with food and lodging. Wagner lived and worked as a deckhand for John until Maren's brother, Ivan, and his wife, Anthe, arrived later that year. After their arrival, Wagner moved to Water Street in Portsmouth, New Hampshire, where he lived in a seedy part of town.

In March 1873, the Hontvet family was thriving on Smuttynose Island. Meanwhile, Louis Wagner faced financial troubles after losing his job on a fishing schooner that had sunk. Desperate and waiting on the docks in Portsmouth on March 5, 1873, he encountered John and Matthew Hontvet, and Ivan Christensen. They informed him that the train carrying their bait had been delayed, forcing them to postpone baiting hundreds of hooks until late into the night.

This left Maren, her sister Karen, and their dog Ringe alone on the island. Wagner knew the family was saving around five hundred dollars for a new boat. His heart raced at the thought of robbing them.

Although he didn't have a detailed plan, the situation seemed perfect for a burglary, as the women would be isolated for a short time. He stole a flat-bottomed boat and, beneath the cover of darkness and, with a sly smile tilting his lips and dreams of fortune blurring his rationality, rowed to Smuttynose Island while the women headed to sleep.

Wagner failed to consider that the barking dog would alert the women inside the tiny wooden home. To his surprise, Karen was visiting and sleeping in the kitchen. With the door left unlocked, Wagner quietly entered the house.

The robbery quickly went awry. Upon discovering Wagner inside, Karen initially mistook him for John. Wagner struck her with a chair and then threw her against a door before turning his attention to Maren when she tried to intervene. Maren temporarily barricaded herself but was unable to save her sister. Meanwhile, Wagner killed Anethe, Maren's sister-in-law, outdoors after she attempted to escape.

Maren ran into the frigid night, hearing Karen scream as the woman was murdered with an axe. After committing these heinous acts, Wagner searched the buildings and property for hours in search of Maren, leaving his bloody boot prints in the snow. Exhausted, he returned to eat before ransacking the house for valuables and fleeing to the mainland. Meanwhile, Maren hid in the snow along the rocky shore until morning and eventually found help from a neighboring island.

Looking disheveled and groggy, Wagner hopped a train to Boston and was quickly apprehended after witnesses identified him based on descriptions provided by local authorities. Wagner's trial commenced on June 9, 1873. After nine days of testimony and just over an hour of jury deliberation, he was found guilty of murder. He managed to escape from jail briefly but was recaptured shortly thereafter.

On June 25, 1875, he was executed by hanging in Thomaston, Maine.

Justice did not stop the ghosts from haunting after the grisly murders. Many visitors report feeling eerie sensations near the site where the slayings occurred. Since that fateful night, the good spirits of Karen and Anethe have lingered on Smuttynose Island. Visitors and locals report hearing their cries and sensing their sorrowful presence. Some have even claimed to see their forms struggling across the remnants of the old home. Their voices still ride the wind, calling out for help.

The ghosts of the ill-fated women are not the only worries for those who visit. There is another ghost that even the least faint-hearted should fear. While it is said that the ghost of Wagner haunts the area out of guilt for the murders, it is more likely that he remains out of outrage for being caught. Those with evil in their hearts rarely change and carry their wickedness even after death.

If you happen to see Wagner's form, as others have, it is wise to leave the area quickly. Something about wickedness can affect even the good if they get too close, wrapping its foul presence around them in a suffocating embrace. This dark influence can pass on a particular depravity even to the purest soul, instilling a touch of misery and rage as a curse that may emerge at the least expected moment—even in your own home.

New Jersey
The Watcher

Do you ever feel as if you are being watched? That prickling sensation creeping along your skin, the shadows shifting as if alive? You glance over your shoulder, your heart racing and the chill deepens. It's as if invisible eyes are watching your every move, waiting... always waiting. Most of the time, this unsettling feeling is just our imagination. But what if, at that moment, you turned around after sensing something and saw the silhouette of a horrifying creature reaching out to snatch at you, only to vanish before you could fully comprehend it?

A family had not a clue they were under the observant eyes of an unknown entity just like this until June 5, 2014, when they checked the mail and found, among a few bills, a white, card-shaped envelope addressed to "The New Owner." Derek and Maria Broaddus had just closed on the shingle-style, six-bedroom house built in 1905 at 657 Boulevard in Westfield, New Jersey, three days earlier. That was when the first letter welcomed the Broadduses to the neighborhood. The letter was from someone identifying themselves as "The Watcher" and said:

Dearest new neighbor at 657 Boulevard,

Allow me to welcome you to the neighborhood.

The letter began in a pleasant tone but quickly became scolding and ominous. The writer chillingly revealed that they had been watching the house for decades, as did generations of family before, and intended to continue by taking a closer look and delving into the family's more private life.

Dearest new neighbor at 657 Boulevard,

Allow me to welcome you to the neighborhood. 657 Boulevard has been the subject of my family for decades now, and as it approaches its 110th birthday, I have been put in charge of watching and waiting for its second coming.

My grandfather watched the house in the 1920s, and my father watched in the 1960s. It is now my time. Do you know the history of the house? Do you know what lies within the walls of 657 Boulevard? Why are you here? I will find out.

Do you need to fill the house with the young blood I requested? Better for me. Was your old house too small for the growing family? Or was it greed to bring me your children? Once I know their names I will call to them and draw them too [sic] me.

There are hundreds and hundreds of cars that drive by 657 Boulevard each day. Maybe I am in one.

Look at all the windows you can see from 657 Boulevard. Maybe I am in one. Look out any of the many windows in 657 Boulevard at all the people who stroll by each day. Maybe I am one.

Welcome my friends, welcome. Let the party begin.

Unnerved, Derek and Maria contacted local law enforcement, who investigated, including searching the home and checking the walls, but could not identify any suspects or trace the letters back to anyone specific in the neighborhood. They also advised the couple not to disclose details about the letters to neighbors, as everyone became a potential suspect. But word of the letters spread, and frightened community members came together, speculating who could be this Watcher.

The couple found out that previous owners, John and Andrea Woods, who had owned the home for 23 years, had received a letter from The Watcher just before they moved out with the writer declaring a close eye was kept on the residence. Believing it was a prank, the letter was tossed into the garbage.

Derek and Maria, because of renovations being done to the dwelling and fearing for the family's safety, had yet to move into the home. Nevertheless, they still brought the children when they were there. However, that stopped immediately. If the first letter was not unsettling enough, a second letter came two weeks later, directly addressed to Derek and Maria Broaddus. The letter contained specific details about their children, including their names and birth order. It spoke about them playing outside and one daughter drawing on the porch, expressing a deep desire to learn more about them. It included a menacing remark about the parents being unable to hear them should they scream.

Welcome again to your new home at 657 Boulevard.

The workers have been busy, and I have been watching you unload carfuls of your personal belongings. The dumpster is a nice touch. Have they found what is in the walls yet? In time, they will.

657 Boulevard is anxious for you to move in. It has been years and years since the young blood ruled the hallways of the house. Have you found all of the secrets it holds yet? Will the young blood play in the basement? Or are they too afraid to go down there alone?

I would [be] very afraid if I were them. It is far away from the rest of the house. If you were upstairs, you would never hear them scream.

Will they sleep in the attic? Or will you all sleep on the second floor? Who has the bedrooms facing the street? I'll know as soon as you move in. It will help me to know who is in which bedroom. Then I can plan better.

All of the windows and doors in 657 Boulevard allow me to watch you and track you as you move through the house. Who am I? I am the Watcher and have been in control of 657 Boulevard for over two decades now. The Woods family turned it over to you. It was their time to move on and kindly sold it when I asked them to.

I pass by many times a day. 657 Boulevard is my job, my life, my obsession. And now you are too Braddus family. Welcome to the product of your greed! Greed is what brought the past three families to 657 Boulevard, and now it has brought you to me.

Have a happy moving in day. You know I will be watching.

After the family decided to delay moving into 657 Boulevard, they stopped taking the children as they feared for their safety. It was well-noted by The Watcher, for they acquired a letter asking where they were. It suggested an increasing sense of urgency from The Watcher regarding their presence in the home.

It merely read:

Where have you gone to? 657 Boulevard is missing you.

It was only six months after the arrival of the first creepy letter that the Broaddus family determined they needed to sell their dream home. They never got to live in it due to The Watcher. But with all the publicity about the strange Watcher and creepy letters, there were no buyers. They even attempted to sell the home to a developer and demolish it. Still, the neighborhood planning board unanimously rejected their request, worrying only about their own investments and how it would lower the value of their homes. Derek and Maria Broaddus ended up renting the property out. And a fourth letter arrived, threatening the Broaddus clan and the new tenants.

The letter read:

To the vile and spiteful Derek and his wench of a wife Maria,

You wonder who The Watcher is? Turn around idiots," the letter read. "Maybe you even spoke to me, one of the so called neighbors who has no idea who The Watcher could be. Or maybe you do know and are too scared to tell anyone. Good move.

657 Boulevard survived your attempted assault and stood strong with its army of supporters barricading its gates... My soldiers of the Boulevard followed my orders to a T. They carried out their mission and saved the soul of 657 Boulevard with my orders. All hail The Watcher!!!

Maybe a car accident. Maybe a fire. Maybe something as simple as a mild illness that never seems to go away but makes you feel sick day after day after day after day after day. Maybe the mysterious death of a pet. Loved ones suddenly die. Planes and cars and bicycles crash. Bones break. You are despised by the house... and The Watcher won.

Despite exhaustive investigations by police, private detectives, and even the FBI, no one was ever unmasked as The Watcher. The letters never stopped. Each one more invasive. More taunting. The kind that makes your skin crawl long after the envelope's been torn open.

After five long years of dread, paranoia, and sleepless nights, the Broadduses gave up. They never moved in. The dream home had become a waking nightmare. They sold the house at a loss—just to escape.

But the house was never what The Watcher wanted.

And The Watcher?

The Watcher is still watching.

They always were.

And perhaps now...

they're watching someone new.

Maybe even you.

Check your mailbox..

New Mexico
The Writhing Dark Lump

Shhhh, don't say it. La Mala Hora. Even mentioning the name aloud can bring bad things. La Mala Hora is dark, sinister, and wicked. It starts as a large, dark lump that wriggles, creeps, and twists until it transforms. Sometimes, it takes the shape of a ghostly shroud or a large black cotton ball. Rarely, it becomes something that resembles a woman floating in the air, her feet never touching the ground. For those who see her in this form, it is considered an omen of death. In this guise, she emerges along lonely and shadowy roads at night, luring passing men. She mesmerizes them.

They do not perceive the evil—perhaps they don't even see beauty. Instead, they feel her charm like the sensation of a first crush, a heart-wrenching longing to be near her. Blinded by this infatuation, they follow her, unaware of the danger she brings. Many men inadvertently find themselves led off cliffs or lost, unable to retrace their steps. The only warning is that her shoes are worn backward. However, most are so enchanted that they fail to notice her unusual footwear, do not realize she is floating, and remain oblivious to the fate that awaits them.

An old story from the Chiapas region recounts the tale of a man walking along a road to visit his girlfriend when he met a beautiful woman resembling her. This woman claimed to have come partway to meet him and expressed a desire to run away together. Captivated by her charm, the man soon noticed that her shoes were worn backward. Realizing her true identity as La Mala Hora, he confronted her. He managed to blindfold her and struck her, which caused her to flee.

The following evening, he returned with a blessed needle and pretended to believe she was his girlfriend again. When they reached a secluded spot, he secretly pricked her with the needle, immobilizing her. He then rushed to find a priest and returned with him at dawn, but La Mala Hora had vanished.

Not long ago, a woman was driving home late at night. Her headlights began to dim as she approached a crossroads, and her car sputtered. An overwhelming sense of dread filled her chest, causing her to freeze in terror. Abruptly, a black shape appeared in the road, writhing and twisting into what she could only describe as a mass that resembled a blobby woman. Trembling, she managed to steer her car around the figure and accelerated, speeding away. Hours later, when she arrived home, she found that at the moment she had encountered the strange shape, her husband had been murdered.

New York
Lady in White of The Devil's Elbow

Nestled between the small towns of Owego and Tioga Center, New York, lies a winding stretch of road affectionately referred to as The Devil's Elbow. This secluded segment of old NY-17C has been a vital artery for travel and commerce for more than two centuries. Its picturesque yet treacherous landscape, characterized by steep inclines and sharp, hairpin turns, has earned it a notorious reputation, resulting in numerous fatal accidents. For the locals who once navigated this route daily before it was straightened a bit by the county, the Devil's Elbow was often a source of frustration and caution.

Adding to the intrigue of this winding road is a ghostly presence reported by many travelers since the 1800s. They recount eerie sightings of a pale woman clad in a flowing white dress resembling either a vintage prom gown or a dress from a bygone era. As these motorists traverse the winding path, they often glimpse her trudging along the roadside, her ethereal figure haunting the periphery of their vision.

Despite her tragic appearance, most drivers choose to pass her by, gripped by a mix of fear and disbelief. Whether driven by urgency or a deep-seated instinct to avoid confrontation with the supernatural, they accelerate, zooming past her without pause. However, those who dare to glance back in their rearview mirrors are met with an unsettling sight—the woman's figure has vanished into thin air, leaving only the twisting road behind, shrouded in mystery and whispers of the past. And sometimes, she is sitting in their backseat.

The ghost's tragic end is somewhat of a mystery that may never be solved. In 1932, near Glenmary Drive at the base of Devil's Elbow Hill, a steam shovel operator cleared the area near a railroad crossing when he unearthed a skull. It was identified as that of a twenty-year-old woman who had lived at least a hundred years earlier. It appeared she had been killed by an axe or blow by a board to the head. The Broadhead Tavern, known for its rough reputation, had been situated nearby in earlier days. In 1925, the old bar was demolished, and a rest stop was later constructed in its place. However, the ghost from its past, although her story may never be revealed, continues on her journey—wherever she is heading—but never wanders far. Some say if you stop there alone, especially after midnight, you might glimpse her in the corner of your eye—a figure in the shadows, standing perfectly still, watching. And if you see her in your rearview mirror...do not look back. Because she's already in the car—

North Carolina
By the Bobbing Brown Mountain Lights

The Blue Ridge Mountains are a smaller segment within the vast Appalachian Mountain range, spanning eight states. These ancient mountains are among the oldest in the world. Brown Mountain is within the Blue Ridge Mountains and Pisgah National Forest near Morganton, North Carolina, and is known for its mysterious phenomenon. Strange lights have been reported floating above Brown Mountain for centuries.

Witnesses have described various colors: red, white, orange, and blue. The lights vary in size, some glowing as faintly as a candle and others as large as a firework rocket. People have seen these lights moving along the forest floor and rising high into the sky.

The lights gained significant attention between 1909 and 1921 when local newspapers began publishing articles about them. Despite extensive research by scientists and organizations such as the Smithsonian, the U.S. Weather Service, and the U.S. Geological Survey, the origin of these lights remains a mystery. Explorations into their unusual appearance have yet to provide a definitive explanation. Some have suggested that the mysterious lights may be phosphorescent light emitted by fungi, known as Will-o'-the-wisp, swamp gas, gases from a rich cache of minerals, or even aliens.

Local legends reveal a secret about these mountains. Long ago, nestled below the rugged cliffs of Brown Mountain, there lived a woman and her husband. The couple kept to themselves, living in isolation from the nearby town, yet they were known to be kind and humble—or so it seemed. However, on a chilly November night, the man was consumed by anger beneath the pale moonlight peeking out from the billowy clouds from an oncoming early winter storm. His obsession with controlling his wife spiraled into madness, culminating in a brutal act of violence. In a fit of rage, he took her life. He left her lifeless body hidden beneath the autumn leaves and the early winter snow, concealed in the remote hollows of the mountain.

But the husband did not realize that the mountain had eyes—eyes that would never allow such wickedness to go unnoticed. The first tiny twinkling light appeared as the wind howled and the wet snow fell thick and fast from the clouds.

It was faint at first, a glimmering spark just above the forest of thick trees. They danced deep within the pockets of scrubby brush on Brown Mountain and over a barely trickling creek. Within hours, more lights began to flicker across the slopes, dancing like tiny, fiery cotton balls, weaving in and out of the forest.

Just before dawn, as the villagers awakened to start their day, they were drawn by the lights. They began to follow them, curious about the strange phenomenon that had started to unfold. The lights led them deep into the mountain, through the dense woodland, over frozen streams, and to the very place where the woman's body lay, cold and lifeless in the snow. The lights shimmered around her, circling her as if mourning her untimely death. The villagers were horrified. They knew instantly what had happened; there were rumors that her husband had grown mad recently.

The lights, it is said, are not of this world. They are the spirits of the mountain, the souls of those who suffered before. Long before the man and woman lived in the little cabin, there was a battle between the Catawba and the Cherokee, fighting over the territory of Brown Mountain. After one bloody clash, women emerged with pine torches, searching vainly for the warriors who never returned. The lights are believed to be the torches of these long-dead phantoms.

They returned to guide the townsfolk to justice for the poor woman. The lights revealed the crime and punished the guilty. Furious, the townspeople dragged the murderer from his cabin, his trembling hands grasping at shadows, his heart a sickening mess of guilt and fear. They hung him for his wickedness, allowing the snow to bury his lifeless body in a grave not of peace but of fury.

Since that day, the twinkling lights have continued to appear, flickering beneath the mountain's crags, silently reminding all who see them that justice is never blind. They emerge when darkness falls, and the air is damp, illuminating the cold, barren landscape like tiny stars in a night sky; their glow can be seen from miles away. The lights dance through the trees, casting a sinister glow across the land, serving as an harbinger for wrongdoers and warning them that they, too, will be exposed—that the mountain will always find them. No secret is safe when the lights guide the innocent to the truth.

And so, when the wind picks up, and the shadows stretch long distances across the town, the people remember, and the rain begins to fall. They know that if lights appear, it's not just a strange phenomenon of nature; it's a call for justice. The mountain sees all, and it never forgets. Those who commit wicked deeds will face the same fate as the murderer—caught, exposed, and punished by the very spirits of the land, led by the eerie glow of the twinkling lights.

North Dakota
Annie Storey: White Lady Lane

In 1921, in the tranquil yet industrious town of Leyden, a spirited 16-year-old named Annie Storey lived in a modest home that bordered the bustling railroad tracks. The rhythmic chug and whistle of the trains provided a constant backdrop to her life, blending the sounds of adventure with the comfort of her familiar surroundings. Within the warm walls of this home were her mother, Matilda, and her two brothers, aged 8 and 11, whose unbridled energy filled the air with joyous laughter and playful chaos.

The ground floor of their residence served as temporary quarters for a wandering peddler named Sam Kalil. He was a man with turbulent thoughts. While the Storeys tucked themselves away in the sanctuary of their upstairs bedrooms as night enveloped their abode, Sam's presence lingered like a shadow below, unnoticed and troubled. One particular evening, under a canopy of stars that seemed to bear witness, Sam's curiosity led him to a troubling discovery. He stumbled upon a cache of letters from Annie to a charming young suitor who had captured her heart. The sweet words flowed with affection and longing, igniting a fierce and consuming jealousy within Sam. Bathed in the moonlight, which cast an eerie glow, he felt gripped by an irrational fixation and quietly ascended the worn wooden stairs. The house remained enveloped in tranquil slumber. Matilda and Annie nestled soundly in their dreams, blissfully unaware of the danger lurking just steps away.

Sam Kalil, filled with rage, softly tiptoed up the stairway, making no sound. He slipped along the hallway and into the room shared by the mother and daughter and shot Annie in the chest with a .33 caliber gun, killing her instantly. Matilda leaped to her feet, her heart pounding and adrenaline coursing through her veins like fire, and she was shot in the cheek. Kalil then fled down the stairs, but Matilda pursued him and wrestled the gun from his hands before anyone else was harmed. The peddler had grabbed a butcher knife and followed the woman upstairs, threatening to kill her.

However, Matilda managed to take the knife from him and tossed it out of the window. Grabbing her son, Matilda sped to Leyden, which was half a mile away, and brought authorities back to her home. Meanwhile, Kahill was sitting on the mattress of the bed next to Annie's corpse and had attempted to kill himself with the butcher knife but had failed poorly.

Sam Kalil was convicted of murder and sentenced to life in Bismarck State Prison. He was released after only ten years, but Annie never saw justice—her fate sealed beneath cold earth. She was laid to rest in Walhalla Hillside Cemetery on November 19, 1921, just beyond the winding road and across the shadowed waters of the Pembina River.

But Annie never truly rested.

They say her spirit still roams the lonely stretches of White Lady Lane and the murky bogs near Eddie's Bridge in Leydon, barefoot, soaked in river water, draped in the same white nightgown she wore the night she died. Travelers have reported seeing her beside the road—weeping, reaching, mouthing silent pleas. Some have followed her, only to vanish.

Those who see her once are cursed to see her again. And if she ever makes it home, someone else will have to take her place.

Ohio

Whistlin' Jack on Moonville Tracks

Once, there were small mining communities, each with a train station, depot, and a few homes for the miners and their families, located along the Marietta and Cincinnati railroad tracks between Zaleski and Athens. This area was remote and wild, with the towns of Moonville, Ingham Station, and Mineral along the straight path of the train tracks that cut through steep hills. Few roads existed along the long stretch, and the area between these towns was dark and isolated. As a result, townspeople and travelers had little choice but to use the tracks to commute to work, buy groceries and supplies, or visit other towns.

In the early 1900s, Ernest Keeton was in his late teens and lived with his family near Moonville. He worked in the mines almost four miles away in Mineral. The young man typically left his job late at night and walked along the dark tracks to get home. He would wake up in the dark in the morning and go to work again. One night, after heading through Mineral City and far from the twinkling lights of the town, he began to hear a strange whistling sound behind him: *thweet-thweet-thweet*. It was high-pitched and squeaky, almost like someone was following him and blowing through a wooden straw.

Ernest paused to see if whatever it was would catch up, craning his neck to look around, but he could not determine the source of the noise. He kept walking but increased his pace. The sound made him uneasy, even though thieves and robbers were uncommon along the tracks. He wasn't worried about being robbed; he didn't have a penny in his pocket. What frightened him were the stories that old-timers told about the Whistlin' Jack. Everyone knew that Whistlin' Jack was said to be a cougar or panther with supernatural powers. It was known to lurk in the woods and let out a strange whistle that sounded like the *thweet-thweet-thweet* he heard. Those curious tended to follow that whistling sound, up the hills and down, gripped by an urge to discover its source. However, those who followed Whistlin' Jack often vanished, never to come out of the dark woods.

The longer Ernest thought about that, the faster he began to walk, continually glancing over his shoulder to see what was following him. Sure enough, after some time, he saw something white, like a sheet, where the whistling was coming from. The White Thing kept perfect pace with him. When Ernest sped up, it sped up. When he slowed down, it slowed down. Then, as he peered over his shoulder again, he noticed the White Thing narrowing the gap between them.

Thweet-thweet-thweet. The Whistlin' Jack was going to get him!

Ernest took off as fast as his boots would carry him, running along the wooden railroad ties and praying he wouldn't trip on the big ballast stones between them. *Thweet-thweet-thweet.* There came a moment when Ernest knew his time was running out. *Thweet-thweet-thweet.* He looked beside him, and the White Thing was keeping perfect pace, side by side, and the whistling sound was growing faster, matching his own panting, frantic breaths. *Thweet-thweet-thweet.* But he made it to the train tunnel just outside Moonville, and as he broke through the threshold, the White Thing disappeared down the embankment. *Thweet-thweet—*

Ernest felt relieved that he had successfully evaded the creature. However, it struck him that the next morning, before dawn, he would have to follow the same tracks in the darkness. After work that night, Ernest would need to turn around and return home. He realized that he had to find out how to avoid the Whistlin' Jack, so he visited one of his gray-haired aunties, who had lived many more years than he had.

"Auntie, I ran into a Whistlin' Jack last night," he told her, even imitating the sound: "*Thweet-thweet-thweet.*" It was a close mimicry. His aunt thought for a moment, tapping her chin. She then pulled out her pipe and lit it with a match.

"You say it made a *thweet-thweet-thweet* sound?" she asked.

"Yeah," he replied.

"And it followed you from Mineral?"

"Yeah."

"And it looked like a white sheet?"

"Yeah."

She took a couple of puffs from her pipe, leaning back with a self-satisfied expression.

"Well, Ernest, that ain't no Whistlin' Jack," she announced. "You don't have to worry about it."

Ernest felt a wave of relief wash over him. "There was a girl named Sarah who died sometime in the 1880s," Aunty said. "She was married for a short time, and one day, she locked herself in the privy..." Aunty crossed her legs, took another puff, and leaned in close to her nephew, "...and slit her throat from ear to ear." Ernest had swallowed hard. "After that, she enjoyed following people down the tracks. She was socializing, I suppose, not realizing she couldn't do that no more after she was dead and all. Yackety, yackety, yackety. She was always a talker. That thweetin' sound you hear isn't Whistlin' Jack, Ernest. That's just the sound the air makes through that dead girl's windpipe after she cut it. It's not a Whistlin' Jack; it's a Whistlin' Sarah," she chuckled. "And she's just a chatty ghost!"

This didn't make Ernest feel any safer—especially with years left walking those haunted tracks alone in the dark. Whether the ghost ever followed him again, no one can say for certain.

But one thing is clear... it still follows others.

You might not see it at first—just a chill crawling up your back, the faint scrape of something dragging behind you, or the whisper of footsteps that stop when you turn around. Or the *thweet-thweet-thweet* sound of air cutting through a corpse's slashed and rotted windpipe.

So, if you ever find yourself walking those tracks after dark... don't look back.

Because if you do, you might finally see who or *what* has been walking just behind you all along.

Oklahoma
Oklahoma City's Crybaby Bridge

Located just beyond the outskirts of Oklahoma City, off East 134th Street, and deep in the tangled underbrush, hidden from the world, lies an old bridge, its rusted frame groaning under the weight of forgotten years. The wooden planks, bleached by time and weather, tremble with each gust of wind as though remembering the horrors they've witnessed. This bridge once spanned the quiet flow of Elm Creek. Still, now, it only leads to an abandoned homestead—nothing more than a decaying foundation, slowly consumed by the earth.

In June 1924, a fierce storm unleashed its wrath as a woman and her baby crossed the bridge in a horse drawn buggy. Thunder rumbled like the growl of some unseen beast, sending the horses into a frenzy. The buggy overturned violently, throwing the woman and child into the chaos. The frantic woman scrambled through the muddy earth, hearing the baby's cries in the deafening storm. She searched for hours—days even—but the baby was never found.

Now, those who dare venture near the bridge, especially on stormy nights, hear the faintest sound—a child's cry, barely audible, drifting on the wind, echoing from somewhere just out of sight. But no one has ever found the source.

And no one ever will.

Oregon
The Bobbysoxer's Ghost

Thelma Taylor was a 15-year-old sophomore at Roosevelt High School. On the morning of August 5, 1949, she was waiting for a bus in the St. Johns neighborhood of Portland. Thelma planned to travel about 17 miles to Hillsboro for a summer job picking beans. She was last seen waiting for the bus on North Fessenden Street in the St. Johns neighborhood, but she never boarded that bus. After she failed to return home, her frantic parents reported her missing, and a police investigation began.

Six days passed with no sign of Thelma until Morris Leland, a 22-year-old drifter with a long criminal history, was arrested for car theft on August 11, 1949. He had a juvenile record and, as an adult, had spent two terms in prison. On his way to the police station, he wanted to speak with homicide detectives. He unexpectedly confessed that he had murdered a girl.

Morris Leland led police to the remains of Thelma, whose broken body was found at the eastern edge of the Willamette River, just two blocks north of the St. John's Bridge on the northern outskirts of Portland. She wore Levi's, a plaid skirt, bobby socks, and brown and white saddle shoes. A small billfold on her body contained a record of Bible school attendance and several work cards she had used for picking farm produce.

The tragic story of Thelma Taylor's death began to unfold when she was waiting for her bus. At around 4:30 p.m., she was approached by Leland, a 22-year-old ex-convict, who lured her to a secluded area near the Willamette River and the St. Johns Bridge. He kept her with him throughout the day and night. Leland became frightened when she refused his advances, thinking that if he let her go, she would create trouble for him, as she was a "good girl."

At 8:00 a.m. the following morning, Leland forced her at knifepoint to walk to some brush along the roadside, taking her to a secluded area near what is now Cathedral Park. As workers at a nearby train yard began their day, Thelma, desperate for help, started screaming. In response, Leland brutally attacked her, striking her twice on the head with a steel bar, and then he stabbed her to silence her cries. Afterward, he buried the young bobbysoxer's body and the weapons he used in a shallow grave under driftwood near the riverbank.

Leland was indicted for first-degree murder on August 19. During his trial, he pleaded not guilty because of insanity. However, on November 11, 1949, he was convicted. Leland received the death penalty and was executed in Oregon's gas chamber on January 9, 1953. He is now condemned to spend eternity in hell. In contrast, Thelma, the victim, remains in the area where she was murdered, endlessly reliving her final moments alive.

On windy nights, blood-curdling screams tear through the silence of the park—disembodied cries that seem to come from nowhere and everywhere at once. Witnesses speak of twisted shadows slithering between trees, replaying some gruesome ritual, as if the kidnapping and murder are trapped in a nightmarish loop, forever clawing to be seen.

Or perhaps Morris Leland has never truly left. Maybe his restless soul, bound by the horrors of what he did, is clawing its way through the very fabric of reality, determined to drag another innocent into his twisted hell. With each passing night, his eyes — those soulless, vacant eyes — grow sharper, more hungry. And as the clock strikes midnight, you can almost hear him whispering in the shadows, waiting... watching... for another young soul to claim.

Don't look too long into the dark.

He might already be closer than you think.

Pennsylvania
Hellhound on his Heels

A quiet dread rippled through a close-knit community in a remote area near Gettysburg in the throes of the dark, cruel winter of 1893—where nearly everyone was bound by blood, marriage, or long-held secrets.

The tension hovered over 18-year-old Emanuel Monn, renting a shabby cabin with 34-year-old Henry Heist on the wooded George Reese property. The dwelling was little more than an old chicken coop in a dark stretch of woods near Maria Furnace, just a stone's throw from the landlord's home.

The two men earned their keep as woodchoppers for a local farmer, Henry Herring. Yet in that desolate stretch of forest, something else hung heavy in the air—something unseen but deeply felt. It wasn't just the isolation or the rustling of branches in the wind. No, this was different. It was a presence, thick and suffocating, like the charged silence before a lightning strike.

Off in the distance, it moved—slowly, deliberately—like a mass of thunderheads crawling across the sky, ink-dark and bloated with menace. It slinked between the trees, unseen but never absent, always at the edge of vision. Every gust of wind carried its weight. Every snapping twig whispered its approach. And with each passing day, it crept closer, drawing near like a storm that would not break… only consume.

And it did. On February 1, 1893, those dark and ominous storm clouds gathered overhead. They seemed to wait and watch with eager, childish delight as if an adult were readying to pass out a sugary treat. It focused on Emanuel and Henry, who were invited to a gathering at the home of Ann and George Reese that evening. The storm eagerly watched, delighting in an argument between Henry and Emanuel, which caused Henry to storm off into the night.

During the altercation, Henry threatened Susanna McCleaf, Reese's daughter and his step-niece, for playfully flirting with Emanuel. Family members observed Emanuel and Susanna sweetly holding hands in the cozy kitchen that night, teasing each other and awkwardly dancing like young people testing the waters of new love often do. The two had even spoken excitedly to Susanna's mother about Emanuel escorting Susanna to visit family on the far side of the mountain near Old Forge in the upcoming week. Henry overheard their conversation. It angered him enough to slap Susanna hard enough to send her across the room.

Not long after Henry stomped off from the Reese home, Emanuel Monn said a quick goodbye. He headed out, indicating that he was returning to his cabin home. Emanuel seemed cheerful and happily played his mouth harp. Unfortunately, that would be the last time his friends and family would see the young Emanuel alive. The storm broke, and Emanuel vanished as if flitting away with those clouds.

After a short time, folks noticed the young man was missing. His father began to ask where his son had gone, as did the nearby families at Maria Furnace. Authorities questioned Henry, but he denied knowing anything. His deceit was not surprising; Henry was not new to this situation and learned how to navigate it—he had already spent time in jail. In 1887, he was convicted of shooting another man, assault, and battery, for which he received a three-year prison sentence. In 1891, authorities jailed him for robbery. He would never confess or provide clues that could incriminate himself. However, he oddly decided to sell everything inside the cabin, including an axe and blanket that belonged to Emanuel Monn.

On March 12, the forest gave up its secret. A search party combing the hillside of Reese's property stumbled upon a shallow grave just 2,185 feet from the cabin Emanuel had once called home. The site was crudely hidden beneath a tangle of brush, jagged rocks, and rotting logs—an unholy cairn masking the horror below.

As they dug, the toe of a boot pierced through the dirt like a rotted finger pointing to the truth. Beneath it lay Emanuel Monn, sprawled on his back in a grotesque stillness. A killer had savagely beaten him so severely that his skull was caved in—crushed with what investigators believed to be a hatchet or hammer. His throat bore a brutal slash, three and a half inches long, likely inflicted while his head was wrenched backward. It wasn't just murder. It was butchery.

Behind his left ear, a series of deep, deliberate blows had cleaved into his brain, leaving the bone shattered like pottery. His windpipe was cleanly severed. His chin—nearly hacked from his face. The grisly murder was not the work of rage alone. It was cold. Calculated. Monstrous.

Emanuel, barely more than a boy, was finally laid to rest in the old Forge Cemetery in Franklin County. But what was buried in that forest was more than just a body. It was the echo of something unspeakable.

Henry fled down the road with a posse on his heels, complete with baying hounds. He managed to elude the law for nearly two months, running desperately through backroads at night and hiding with family during the day. Ultimately, he had run out of places to hide. Exhausted and rejected by those who would no longer offer him shelter, he surrendered to the police in Gettysburg.

On January 17, 1894, the executioner carried out the hanging of Henry Heist in Gettysburg. No family came to collect the body. No friends spoke his name. The county laid him in the potter's field near the county home—buried in shame and silence. A cold marble slab marked his resting place with his name, his date of death, and a single damning word: "HUNG." But even that could not rest in peace. Sometime later, no one knows who chiseled the word off the stone. It was futile as if erasing it could cleanse the horror.

But Heist did not stay buried.

They say he rose again—not in the flesh, but in a darker form. Forever cursed, forever hunted. His was the final execution in Adams County, a grim milestone in Gettysburg's long and blood-soaked past. Yet his punishment had only just begun.

After his death, something settled over Maria Furnace Road. A shadow. A silence.

People began avoiding the winding forest paths that cut south and west of the old site, especially in winter, when the air hung cold and still. Whispers told of a figure drifting between the trees—gaunt, limping, hollow-eyed. They say it was Heist, cursed to roam where his sins were born.

But he was not alone.

On frigid nights, ghostly hounds would rise from the earth, their howls echoing through the black woods. They didn't hunt him for justice in this world—they had no interest in trials or gallows. These were the hounds of the beyond, relentless and otherworldly, sent to drag his tormented soul down, past the grave, past mercy, into something far worse. They chased him still, night after night, gnashing through the frost-covered leaves, ensuring he would never escape the justice waiting for him in the deep, deep depths of hell.

Rhode Island
Gruesome Tale of the Palatine Light

In the winter of 1738, the ship Princess Augusta was transporting about 340 passengers, primarily German immigrants known as Palatines, across the Atlantic Ocean from Rotterdam to Philadelphia. A fierce winter snowstorm battered the already treacherous seas. The journey appeared to be destined for failure. Supplies dwindled, and disease began to spread among the passengers due to contaminated water. During the voyage, 200 passengers and half the crew, including the captain, died, leaving First Mate Andrew Brook in command.

Unfortunately, he started extorting the remaining provisions from those on board. On December 27, 1738, the ship ran aground on a sandbar off the northern coast of Block Island, Rhode Island, due to a powerful snowstorm.

Local islanders assisted the survivors who sought refuge on the island; however, some individuals looted the ship and got into scuffles with the already sick and suffering passengers. First Mate Andrew Brook fled the scene, abandoning those still on board. The local residents were concerned about the potential spread of disease to their community. To prevent any health risks and eliminate what they perceived as a threat from the wrecked vessel, they decided to burn the remains of the ship. And so it burned, a fierce blaze consuming every inch. Yet, from the ashes, it was not truly gone. A haunting reminder of its tragic end lingered, a sinister legacy for those who dared to set flame to her decks.

Not long after the wreck, an eerie light began to haunt the waters where Princess Augusta met her end between Christmas and New Year's Eve. Locals watched in fear as a ghostly glow—flickering like flames—rose from the sea, dancing above the black waves. It swelled and shrank without warning, pulsing with unnatural life. Sometimes it hovered near the shore; other times, it loomed miles out like a beacon for the damned.

But it was no guide.

For generations, sailors have steered their ships far from the cursed glow known as the Palatine Light, named after the place the ill-fated passengers came, whispering that its appearance foretells more than storms—it marks death. Ships that veered too close vanished into the mist. Survivors spoke of a pressure in the air, of the cold biting deeper than it should, and of voices—wailing, pleading—rising from the deep and seeming to never end.

Most chilling is the tale of Mary Vanderline, a young passenger said to have gone mad in the final hours of the doomed voyage. Trapped by terror and desperation, she refused to abandon the burning ship, clinging to her few earthly possessions as fire licked across the deck. Witnesses claimed to hear her screams as the vessel was set adrift—shrill, animal cries that pierced the howling wind.

To this day, on winter nights when the tide is low, and the light is seen, her shrieks return—echoing across Block Island's cliffs and beaches, carried on the sea like a dying woman's curse. Some say she's still there, trapped in the flames, her soul fused to the ship's ghostly shell—burning, screaming, and forever sinking.

South Carolina
Gray Man's Doom on Pawleys Island

Along the windswept beaches and whispering dunes of Pawleys Island, South Carolina, a ghost walks when the storm is near. Locals call him the Gray Man—a silent, spectral figure said to appear just before hurricanes make landfall. He does not speak. He does not stay. But those who see him know what follows: devastation. The legend of the Gray Man stretches back over two centuries, first recorded in 1822 and passed down like a whispered warning from one generation to the next. Yet, its origins were not so ominous.

The tale begins with Plowden C.J. Weston, a wealthy and influential landowner who built a grand estate on the windswept shores of Pawleys Island in the 1800s. He was known for his intelligence and ambition—but more than anything, he was known for the depth of his love for his wife, Emily Esdaille Weston. Their bond was said to be unbreakable, the kind that bends the laws of life and death.

But death came anyway.

In 1864, Plowden was claimed by tuberculosis—a slow, agonizing descent that left Emily shattered. Alone in the vast, echoing halls of their seaside home, she drifted through grief like a ghost herself. But soon, whispers began—unsettling, impossible whispers. Emily confided in those closest to her and said she was not alone.

She had seen *him*.

Not in dreams or memories but with waking eyes.

Plowden, pale and distant, walking the beach just beyond the dunes. Always at dusk. Always in his gray coat—the one he had worn so often in life. His footsteps left no prints in the sand. The wind didn't move his hair. And his face... was not the face she remembered. Neighbors spoke in hushed tones of the widow on the beach, standing in the mist, calling out to someone no one else could see. Of a gray figure watching from the water's edge, vanishing when approached. The haunting grew stronger—lights flickering in the Weston home long after it had been boarded up, strange cries in the dead of night, and the chilling sound of footsteps pacing the porch when the tide rolled in.

To this day, locals say Plowden never indeed left Pawleys Island. His love tethered him there—or perhaps it was something darker. Something unfinished. Some nights, when the fog clings low, and the ocean falls unnaturally still, people see him wandering the shore... silent, searching... waiting.

And if you're walking alone after dark, you might catch a glimpse too—just ahead, in the mist. A man in a gray coat who was buried long ago. Yet, you may not want to see him. According to legend, his haunting image brings doom.

For it is not just a tale but a prophecy embedded in the bones of the island. Now, he returns when the sea is restless. His presence is a warning—a final act of love or regret, no one knows. Those who witness the Gray Man are considered the fortunate few. Their homes often stand untouched when others fall to ruin. Clara and Jim Moore, survivors of Hurricane Hugo in 1989, claimed to have seen him before the storm struck. Their home, miraculously, was spared while destruction rained down around them.

But the Gray Man does not appear to all. Only those who need to see him. Only those who are willing to believe.

Some say his feet never touch the ground. Others claim the air grows cold in his wake and that a whisper rides the wind just before he vanishes—"Leave."

And when he's gone, the sea begins to rise.

South Dakota
Hooky Jack

John Leary was born in 1849 in Newburgh, New York—but the story that earned him a place in legend began far from home, in the shadowed hills of South Dakota. At just sixteen, he chased the gold fever westward to the Black Hills, settling near the Old Grand Junction Mine in Custer City. There, fate took its price. While trying to thaw frozen explosives with his bare hands, the charges detonated—instantly mangling his arms and leaving him horrifically disfigured.

But John didn't die. He came back with steel.

He had special iron hooks fashioned to replace his lost hands—cold, gleaming things that clacked when he walked. Locals began to call him "Hooky Jack." His gait was unmistakable: a slow, dragging shuffle through the streets of Rapid City, the metallic ring of his prosthetic arms echoing off the walls of sleeping buildings. *Thump-thump-sssst.*

Despite his appearance, Jack was a fixture of the town, serving as its night watchman for over four decades. He was a strange figure of comfort and unease—offering cheerful "good mornings" with a grin carved by time and pain, his lifeless hooks occasionally reaching for a doorknob to ensure the city slept safely, *click-click.*

But even in life, his presence was unsettling. Boys, drawn by mischief and morbid curiosity, once hung him by his own hooks from a street post—his body swinging in the moonlight like a broken clock. When he was found, those boys were punished publicly... but some whispered that Hooky Jack never entirely moved the same again.

His only companion was a terrier named Rags. Half-blind and trembling, the dog kept its face pressed to Jack's trouser leg as though sensing something no one else could—something colder than the November wind that would one day take his master. On a gray, bitter day in 1926, Hooky Jack met his end under the wheels of a motor car on Main Street near the fire station. The city mourned—but it seems Jack never really left.

Since his death, chilling reports have surfaced. On certain nights, especially in late autumn when the air grows sharp, and the streets fall quiet, people claim to see a hunched figure gliding through the dark with noisy feet still tromping the ground in his well-known dragging-foot shuffle. *Thump-thump-sssst.* They hear the metallic *tap-tap-tap* of hooks on brick and the soft, shuffling steps of a man long buried.

A scent of iron and smoke lingers in the air. And some swear they hear a hoarse voice, far off in the dark, wishing them a gentle "good morning."

But the eerie part lies in the silence that follows—and the cold, invisible hand that sometimes brushes against the doorknobs... just before it turns *click-click*. Is it Hooky Jack still going about his tasks? Or is it someone or *something* more sinister?

Tennessee
Trapped

Tucked deep within a shadowed hollow that winds beneath Mount LeConte and stretches toward Gatlinburg once lay the forgotten hamlet of Spruce Flats. Surrounded by dense forest and cloaked in perpetual mist, the village had everything it needed to sustain itself—a modest schoolhouse, a weather-worn church, a mill that never stopped turning, and a general store where gossip passed more often than coins.

Families like the Bales, Reagans, Ogles, Clabos, and Mellingers called Spruce Flats home. They lived close to the land—and even closer to one another. But something dark once took root, a shadow that no season could wash away.

The Mellinger name, once spoken with warmth and familiarity, became tethered to something far more sinister. Jasper and Martha Mellinger lived in a two-room cabin on a 30-acre homestead along the Roaring Fork. Their property featured a vegetable garden, a cornfield, and a barn with pasture for livestock. Jasper farmed and worked as a blacksmith for additional income. Despite the challenges, the family of four managed to get by. But a disappearance—sudden, unexplained, and soaked in silence—rattled the community to its core.

Some still say it was murder. Others believe the land itself swallowed Jasper Mellinger whole. But whatever truth lies beneath, it was never uncovered. And in the stillness of Spruce Flats, where the wind sounds almost like weeping, and the forest grows a little too thick, that absence still lingers—watchful, waiting.

In the harsh winter of 1901, Martha watched her husband Jasper leave their homestead searching for work. At 64, he headed toward Hazel Creek, North Carolina, twenty-four miles away, hoping to find blacksmith jobs in the nearby copper mine camps as they needed extra cash. The path he had to traverse was perilous, winding through steep, rocky mountains and cliffs. It might take him more than two weeks to complete his journey. That was the last time she saw Jasper; he did not return. For years, there was no trace left behind. Just a house gone cold overnight and memories that began to leave through the chimney like smoke from an unseen fire.

Four long years passed after the mysterious disappearance of Jasper Mellinger—four years of unanswered questions and sleepless nights for those who remembered his kind eyes and soft-spoken nature. Then, as if summoned by the weight of his secrets or hearing the growls of the hellhounds sniffing outside his door, a young man from Wear's Valley lay dying.

Fevered and restless, he begged to speak before his soul left this world. What he confessed chilled the blood of all who listened.

Years earlier, he and his father, John Beasley, had been setting illegal bear traps deep within the forest—no warning signs, no markers—just cold, rusted steel jaws hidden in the trail's underbrush. When they returned to check the traps, they found not an animal but a man. His leg was mangled, caught deep in the iron teeth. He had died there alone, starved, frozen, a look of silent horror still clinging to the ice-rimmed skin of his face.

They recognized what they had done. And they feared what the law would do in return. So, they said nothing. No burial. No prayer. Just silence. They covered the broken body with branches and left the man to rot beneath the trees—forgotten, they hoped, by both the world and whatever lies beyond it.

But the dead do not forget. When word of the dying man's confession reached a nearby family who had last seen Jasper alive, bedding down near Cold Knob—they set out into the wilderness. The search led them to a rifle with the initials "J.M." crudely carved into the stock. Nearby: a rusted pocket watch, three coins dulled by weather, and scattered bones—picked clean by time and beasts. The family collected the rotting remains, returning them to Spruce Flats, where they were buried on a mountainside above the Roaring Forks Motor Trail in the Smokies.

Some say Jasper was already dead when the trappers found him. Others swear—by candlelight and trembling breath—that the trappers found him alive, and it was a club to the head that ended him. There are still a few, older than the rest, who mutter that Jasper's death was not at the hands of man at all—but something far older and darker that haunts those woods beneath Cold Knob and traps those who wander through.

The younger Beasley was already gone, buried by fever, taken by the hounds, and dragged to hell. The father was arrested, tried, and—by the cruel hand of fate—released to go. Regardless, justice, it seems, was never fulfilled. Jasper Mellinger can never rest. They say that on nights when the wind howls through the trees and the hemlocks sway like mourners at a grave, a pale figure limps through the trail heading for home, dragging a bloodless leg behind him. Traps, long and rusted, still snap without warning. The air grows cold. And from somewhere in the trees, a voice—thin, broken, and laced with sorrow—cries out for help that never came.

Jasper Mellinger is still out there. His restless spirit wanders in the dark corners of the night, a specter driven by an insatiable thirst for justice—and revenge. He has no mercy, no peace, and no destination but the man who took his life. His eyes burn with an otherworldly hunger, seeking the one who betrayed him.

If you should see him, pray he does not mistake you for the one who brought him down.

Texas
Old Ghost Road

A lonely stretch of dirt road is carved through a swamp near Saratoga, Texas. Locals know it as Bragg Road, but Ghost Road is the name whispered most often—and never after dark. It is just 7.8 miles long, but every inch of it hums with something ancient and unnatural. Travelers swear it's the longest road they've ever dared to roam, and some never make it to the end.

Many years ago, during the Texas oil boom, this pathway was a bustling railroad spur—hauling men, machines, and crude resources through the heart of the Big Thicket.

But by 1934, the rails were torn up and forgotten, leaving only the bones of the track beneath the muck. Nature began to reclaim what man had abandoned, but something else... darker... remained.

Since the early 1900s, an eerie, glowing light appears along this road. It's no trick of the eye or flash of lightning—this light moves purposefully. It bobs and dances, weaving through the trees like it's alive. It suddenly appears, hovers without sound, and vanishes when you think you're safe. Some say it follows. Others say it waits.

According to legend, that light belongs to the ghost of a railroad conductor—a man who met a gruesome end in a violent accident on the very tracks that once ran through the swamp. His body was found twisted and mangled beneath the train wheels. His head, however, was never recovered.

Now, his restless spirit wanders Ghost Road, eternally bound to that place of blood and metal, swinging a lantern in his cold, skeletal grip—searching, always searching, for the head that was taken from him.

Those who dare to walk or drive down Bragg Road after dark report more than just the floating light. They speak of the oppressive silence, broken only by the phantom clatter of invisible train wheels, the sharp whistle of a locomotive that no longer exists, and sometimes... breathing. Not their own.

There have been reports of cars mysteriously stalling, of headlights dying all at once, of shapes moving in the treetops—and worst of all, the sudden appearance of the conductor himself. Faceless, headless, the stump of his neck slick with ghostly blood, standing in the middle of the road, arm raised high, lantern glowing like a dying star.

If you see the light, do not follow it. Do not call out. Do not stop. Because the conductor is still looking. And he might mistake your head for the one he lost.

Utah
Ghoul of the Great Salt Lake

In the chill of a Utah winter, January 17, 1862, 25-year-old Moroni Clawson died under a cloud of violence and scandal. The young Mormon pioneer entangled in crime was shot while allegedly trying to escape custody after being arrested for assaulting Governor John W. Dawson—a political figure who fled Utah under a storm of hostility. Clawson died alone. No family stepped forward to claim his body. No friends mourned. Only Officer Henry Heath, out of pity or duty, bought burial clothes and saw that the young man was laid to rest in the cold, forsaken soil of a potter's field.

But death was not the end.

Weeks later, Clawson's elder brother George obtained permission to exhume the body and rebury him in the family plot. But when the grave was opened, horror rose with the stench of disturbed earth and rotted flesh. Moroni Clawson's corpse was stripped bare, face down in the coffin, as though flung within without regard. His burial clothes were gone.

The investigation led Officer Heath to the man tasked with tending the city's dead: 49-year-old Jean Baptiste, a quiet, watchful gravedigger whose work went unquestioned—until now. When officers entered Baptiste's home, they uncovered a hidden chamber of nightmares.

Boxes. Dozens of them. When Baptiste's home was investigated, authorities discovered stacks of boxes filled with stolen burial clothing and other items taken from over 300 graves, including neatly folded burial clothes, almost 60 pairs of child's and adult's shoes, and personal belongings.

When word spread, Salt Lake City erupted in outrage. Families of the dead screamed and wept, crowding the courtrooms demanding answers. But how could one explain such blasphemy? Families were so distraught that Brigham Young came forward and tried to soothe the loved ones of the dead, ensuring them that those buried would rise up in the resurrection wearing the original clothes in which they were buried. Meanwhile, a great box of the dead's clothing was buried in a communal grave, a symbolic gesture for peace—but the wound it left never truly closed.

The punishment for Jean Baptiste, the graverobber, which at the time were called ghouls, would not be jail or death but exile. Branded with "GRAVE ROBBER" across his forehead, Baptiste was ferried to Great Salt Lake's Antelope Island and later to more distant Fremont Island, alone with only meager provisions and the company of his damned conscience.

But evil rarely dies quietly. When officials returned just three weeks later, they found his shelter dismantled, a cow slaughtered, and no sign of Baptiste. He had vanished—perhaps drowned, perhaps fled across the lake on a raft of bone and hide, possibly claimed by the dead themselves.

Years passed. In 1893, a duck hunter found a skeleton shackled with an iron ball near the Great Salt Lake—its jaw frozen in a final scream. Many believed it was Baptiste, though some insisted it belonged to another escaped prisoner from the penitentiary. The truth was never found, and Baptiste's fate became a riddle carved into the salt and wind.

To this day, along the haunted shores of Fremont Island and in the dusk mists of Antelope State Park, visitors report a hunched figure wandering the shoreline, dragging something behind him—chains, perhaps... or guilt. They say he digs still, searching for the dead he once desecrated, hoping to return what he stole and earn forgiveness that will never come.

Vermont
What Anna Saw

Mildred Brewster was just twenty years old—a quiet seamstress known to take on odd jobs around Montpelier, Vermont, a small but vibrant city characterized by its role as the state capital and bustling commercial activities. She boarded on Barre Street, living simply, with little to her name. But what she had, she poured into a secret, smoldering love for a man named Jack Wheeler, a stonecutter at the Fraser & Broadfoot granite sheds.

The trouble was—Jack was already promised to another—seventeen-year-old Carrie "Anna" Wheeler, delicate and cheerful, who worked as a domestic servant and lived with her cousins, the Bugbees, on East Liberty Street. Jack's affections, it seemed, had been shared between the two women. Their rivalry simmered for months until it reached a breaking point on the morning of May 29, 1897.

That morning, Anna dressed her best, preparing to meet her fiancé at 8:30 a.m. on a train headed to the Decoration Day festivities. Meanwhile, just blocks away, Mildred stood alone with a newly purchased .32 caliber revolver, practicing her aim in the early light. Her mind was made up.

Witnesses saw Mildred arrive at the Bugbee house. The two women spoke in hushed tones on the porch. One neighbor later claimed she heard Mildred say, "He cannot have us both. He must choose."

And then—they left. Together. Sharing a black umbrella, they walked quietly down College Street under the cloud-covered sky. They were last seen cutting across the tall grass of a field, making their way toward Jack's home on Sibley Avenue.

Only one of them would return.

As they neared the edge of the field, Mildred stopped. She turned to Anna. In a single, chilling moment, she raised the revolver and fired point-blank into Anna's head. Then, without hesitation, she turned the weapon on herself.

Anna was rushed to Heaton Hospital, where she died at 1:30 p.m. Mildred survived. Her trial nearly a year later captivated the state. She claimed madness. The jury believed her. She was found not guilty because of insanity and vanished behind the walls of asylums for decades.

But Anna never left.

According to locals, her spirit still lingers on the grounds of what is now the Vermont College of Fine Arts. In the bell tower—formerly the Montpelier Seminary and now known as College Hall—doors have been reported to slam shut without human hands to turn a knob. The bell tower was the last thing she saw before collapsing to the ground, unconscious, and it is the tower she remembers and returns to. Footsteps echo through empty rooms. Objects vanish and reappear. Cold air coils around ankles.

And sometimes, if you listen closely on quiet nights, just before the hour strikes—

You'll hear a soft voice whisper, "He must choose."

But he never did. And so Anna waits. Forever watching. Forever walking. Forever wronged.

Virginia
Few Return Twice

In 1750, explorer Thomas Walker carved his way through the wilds of the Appalachian frontier, charting what would become known as the Cumberland Gap—a deep, shadowed pass where Kentucky, Tennessee, and Virginia now meet. Among his findings, Walker marked a gaping mouth in the mountainside—a cavern of unknowable depth, which he called Gap Cave. It was a place of strange echoes and breathless stillness, where even the bravest scout lingered no longer than necessary.

By 1819, the spring that surged from the cave's depths was harnessed to power sawmills, gristmills, and the iron blast machinery of the Cumberland Iron Works. A small settlement emerged, huddled close to the cave's yawning entrance like it sought protection—or perhaps dared not stray too far.

It wasn't long before the miners came, descending into the cold dark to carve saltpeter from the earth. And then the war arrived.

During the Civil War, Gap Cave became more than a hollow in the rock—it became a sanctuary and a tomb. The lower chamber, King Solomon's Cave, served as a storehouse. The upper chamber, Soldier's Cave, was used as a makeshift hospital. There, in the choking dark, wounded men were laid on the cold stone, their cries peeling out into the dark interior. Many did not leave.

Not all were accounted for when the war ended, and the soldiers left. Something remained.

For generations, those who dared wander into the depths of Gap Cave have reported encounters with a ghostly figure—a heavy-set man clad in the tattered remains of a Confederate officer's uniform. His boots echo where no footfalls should be heard. His long, gray beard hangs to his belly, matted and motionless, and his eyes are hollow sockets—not blind, but watching.

He stands still as if waiting for orders that will never come.

They say if you venture too far into Soldier's Cave alone, you'll feel a sudden drop in temperature and hear labored breathing—not yours, but coming from just behind your shoulder. Some speak of hearing a low growl or the sound of boots scraping across stone. And those who have seen his face say it bears the look of a man who has not only died—but remembered it. Over and over again.

Few return twice. Because once you've seen him, he's seen you too. And some believe that when the cave grows still again, he follows.

Washington
Thousand Steps

Tucked into the shadowed hills of Spokane, a weathered stone stairway winds its way into darkness. Locals call it the Thousand Steps, though there are only sixty—sixty narrow, crumbling stairs that seem to stretch much farther than they should. Flanked by overgrown brush and twisted trees, the path feels more like a forgotten tunnel than a trail. Sunlight rarely reaches here. It's always dim, always still.

At the very top, like an ancient sentinel watching the living approach, stands the decaying husk of an old mausoleum.

Its iron door is rusted shut, and its nameplate is long and worn and smoothed by time and weather. The steps end at Greenwood Cemetery, a place whispered about in hushed tones, especially after dark.

As visitors ascend the stairs, many report seeing pale figures lingering just a few steps ahead—motionless silhouettes cloaked in shadows, vanishing if approached. Some say these figures stare down from the brush. Others claim they reach out as if to drag trespassers back into the silence of the earth.

Once within the cemetery, the air turns cold and heavy. People speak of being touched by unseen hands, fingers that graze their shoulders or brush their necks with ice-cold precision. Cameras malfunction. Footsteps echo when no one else is there. And some who make the climb say they hear whispers calling their name—from beneath the steps.

It may only be sixty steps, but each one pulls you deeper into something older than the cemetery itself—something that waits at the top, in the dark, to be noticed. Or worse— remembered.

West Virginia
The Mothman

On a bleak November 12, 1966, under a leaden sky, Kenneth Duncan stood alone in a Clendenin cemetery, digging a grave for his father-in-law. As the wind stirred the brittle leaves, something moved above the treetops. Kenneth looked up—and froze. Hovering just above the canopy was a dark, winged figure, humanoid, but wholly unnatural. He described it later as a "brown human being with wings." It watched him silently for nearly a minute before vanishing without a sound. The others with him saw nothing. But Kenneth knew—it wasn't a bird. It was something else. And it was watching.

That eerie encounter was only the beginning. Just days later, on November 15, four young adults—Steve and Mary Mallette and Roger and Linda Scarberry—cruised through the ruins of the TNT Area near Point Pleasant. Once a sprawling wartime munitions factory, it had become a crumbling relic, riddled with overgrown trails, decaying bunkers, and hollow silence. It was nearly midnight when the headlights of Roger's 1957 Chevy cut through the darkness—and revealed something inhuman.

A hulking shape stumbled across the road. Linda Scarberry would later tell police, "It didn't run. It wobbled like it couldn't quite remember how to walk. Its wings were spread—just a little. Enough to know they were there."

Steve, an experienced hunter, caught a glimpse of the creature's eyes first—six inches apart, glowing red like embers, peering through the brush. And then it moved again. As the car sped down the road, the creature followed—not running, but gliding, silently, malevolently. It kept pace with the speeding car at over 100 miles per hour. Its massive wings cast shadows over the vehicle, and a high-pitched screech— not quite animal, not quite mechanical—pierced the night. It wasn't chasing them. It was playing with them.

Roger described it as "six feet tall, light grey, man-shaped... but with wings like a demon and eyes like burning coals." Linda claimed the wings scraped the sides of the car, leaving claw-like scratches in the paint. They didn't stop until they were deep in town, hearts pounding, headlights illuminating nothing but empty road.

That same night, the group returned to the TNT area with Deputy Millard Halstead. But the creature was not done with them. As they sat in silence, a powerful static hum filled the air. A shadow passed across the hill, and then—those same burning red eyes glowed once again from the darkness.

The deputy's spotlight caught nothing but rising dust... and the sense that something was still watching, still waiting.

Word of the encounter spread quickly. Locals scoffed, blaming owls, cranes, even weather balloons. But the witnesses stood firm. "It wasn't a bird," Roger said. "It was watching us. It wanted us to see it."

That same month, two bikers—Bob Bosworth and Alan Coates—took a shortcut through the TNT Area. As they neared the crumbling power plant, they saw a shape perched high on the roof. They tilted their headlight up, but the thing didn't move. So, drawn by equal parts fear and curiosity, they entered the building.

Up on the third floor, among the rusted catwalks, they saw it. A figure nearly seven feet tall, its wings folded tightly against its back, silently walking toward them. There was no sound—no footsteps, no breath—only a suffocating stillness. And then, without warning, the creature lifted into the air and vanished into the night, swallowed by the dark.

It wasn't a prank. It wasn't a bird.

Something had been unearthed in that old wartime ruin—something ancient, unnatural, and watching.

And in the months to come, Point Pleasant would learn what it means to be haunted.

In the following weeks, the sightings intensified—more glowing eyes in the dark, more wings brushing through the trees above empty roads, more unsettling encounters whispered about behind closed doors. Then came December 15, 1967. Without warning, the Silver Bridge connecting Point Pleasant to Gallipolis, Ohio, crumbled during rush-hour traffic. Forty-six people plunged into the frigid waters of the Ohio River. Rescue efforts turned into recovery missions.

Though the official cause was a microscopic fracture in a single eyebar—overlooked, fatigued, and stressed by years of use—locals believed something far darker had been at play. In the days before the collapse, Mothman had been seen repeatedly, perched high on the bridge's steel beams, its burning red eyes fixed on the town below. After the tragedy, the creature vanished as suddenly as it had appeared.

To this day, many believe that Mothman was never meant to harm—but to warn. A spectral sentinel that emerges before a catastrophe, its wings shadowing those who are fated to perish. Some say that if you see the Mothman, it's already too late. Others say it's still out there, waiting for the next collapse, the next scream in the dark, the next moment when the ordinary world splits open and something ancient peers through.

And the red eyes return.

Wisconsin
Bloody Bride Bridge

There is a bridge on Highway 66 near Jordan Park in Stevens Point, Wisconsin—a place locals speak of in hushed tones, especially when the sky turns gray and sleet starts to fall. Beneath its rusted guardrails and crumbling concrete lies a story soaked in blood, sorrow, and something that will not rest.

Years ago, a young couple was enroute to their wedding, navigating the winding road through a brutal winter storm. The sleet fell like shards of glass, and visibility was nearly zero.

As they approached the bridge, the car lost control. It spun, collided, and finally crumpled against the icy railing. The bride-to-be was thrown violently from the vehicle, her white gown instantly stained red as her body skidded across the frozen pavement.

The groom, bloodied and dazed, staggered from the wreckage—only to witness something he would never forget. He claimed that her body, twisted and broken, rose from the road. Or rather, something ripped away from it. "It wasn't just her," he later muttered to authorities. "It was like her soul... tore itself out of the corpse. She stood up, looked right at me with dead, empty eyes... then turned and walked off into the dark. But when I looked down again—she was still there. Still dead at my feet."

Since that night, those who cross the bridge after dusk— especially in the cold grip of winter—tell of a spectral woman wandering the span in a blood-drenched wedding gown. Her veil drips as though soaked, her face twisted in eternal anguish, her movements jerky, unnatural. She doesn't walk... she glides as if half tethered to the earth, half being dragged back into it.

One of the most disturbing accounts comes from a seasoned police officer who believed he had struck a woman standing in the middle of the bridge. His car jolted violently, and he slammed the brakes, heart pounding. But when he climbed out, there was nothing—no body, no blood, no evidence of a collision. Relieved, if only slightly, he returned to his cruiser... only to find her sitting silently in the backseat, staring at him through the rearview mirror. When he turned around—she was gone.

Fishermen who cast their lines in the river beneath the bridge before dawn or after dusk often report an unbearable weight in the air, as if eyes are crawling across their skin.

Some claim to hear whispers beneath the rush of the current. Others say they've seen a white figure hovering just beneath the water's surface, eyes wide open, mouth frozen mid-scream.

And the legend doesn't end there. Locals warn: never look into your rearview mirror as you cross the bridge. If you do, you may see her—sitting in the backseat, her face pale and bloodied, veil fluttering in an unseen wind. Sometimes, she screams. Other times, she simply stares... waiting for someone to join her.

Once you've seen her, the legend says, you'll see her again. And again. Until it's your turn to have your soul ripped out of your body on that cursed bridge.

Wyoming
Runaway Ghost Train of Cheyenne

On the eve of August 3, 1950, at precisely 6:55 p.m., Union Pacific locomotive No. 820 was called into service from the rail yards in Cheyenne, Wyoming. Its assignment was routine—assist a passenger train over the unforgiving incline of Sherman Hill, a treacherous stretch of track 31 miles west. The locomotive completed its task and was detached at the summit, drifting back east toward the lonely outpost of Borie.

By 9:00 p.m., No. 820 stood unobtrusively on the eastbound track at Borie, left unattended in the waning twilight.

183

The engineer briefly stepped away to take a call from the control tower. The fireman moved to place warning signals down the line. Neither could have known what was about to happen.

Just five minutes later, with no crew aboard and no orders given, No. 820 began to move with a life of its own.

Witnesses say there were no sounds of ignition, no slow churning of gears—just the sudden metallic scream of steel grinding against steel as the engine began to move. It gained speed quickly as if something unseen now guided it with purpose... or fury. Hurtling eastward, it barreled toward Cheyenne—toward Union Pacific locomotive No. 1149, which was traveling 70 miles per hour and pushing freight cars into the roundhouse area in town.

The collision was apocalyptic.

The impact tore both engines to pieces. The metal twisted and crumpled. Chaos erupted from the mangled wreckage. The engineer, his fireman, and a switchman were instantly killed—what remained of their bodies was found scattered in the debris field, unrecognizable, crushed, and broken.

In the aftermath, railroad officials tried to explain the incident. Employee failure, miscommunication, a brake left unsecured. But behind closed doors, there were whispers about what the men on the scene saw in the moments before the impact. Some swore they heard the haunting blare of a whistle echoing in the night, one that didn't belong to any engine currently in service. Others claimed that, just before the crash, the signal lights along the track turned green—on their own. Then came the reports. Locals began to hear phantom trains—roaring past in the darkness with no headlights and no wheels on the track. Crossings would clang to life in the dead of night, warning of a ghostly engine that never appeared. Lights blinked frantically at crossings.

Whistles screamed from nowhere.

Even more chilling, some claim that if you stand near the site of the accident at around 9:22 p.m.—the time of the crash—you can hear the sounds of twisting metal and distant screams. A low rumble in the earth and the mournful wail of a train that should no longer exist.

They say Engine 820 never stopped that night.

It just vanished into the wreckage... and now rides the rails alone. A runaway ghost, forever replaying the moment of its deadly descent. And sometimes, when the wind is right, you can still hear it coming.

Citations

Alabama:

Abbeville Herald Abbeville, Alabama Thu, Nov 17, 2005 Page 6

Alaska:

Daily Sitka Sentinel Sitka, Alaska Tue, Oct 31, 1989 Page 1

Colp, H. D. (1953). *The strangest story ever told*.

Arizona:

https://www.familysearch.org/ark:/61903/1:1:FLVN-S28?lang=en

The Modesto Bee Modesto, California Tue, May 8, 1928 Page 5

https://www.findagrave.com/memorial/148108654/leone-i-jensen

The Arizona Republic Phoenix, Arizona Tue, May 8, 1928 Page 4

Arkansas:

Madison County Record Huntsville, Arkansas January 16, 1930 Page 2

California:

San Francisco Examiner San Francisco, Cal August 17, 1896 Page 12

Colorado:

The Daily Sentinel Grand Junction, Colorado Fri, April 26, 1907 Page 1

Second Alfred Packer confession. (n.d.). Retrieved from gunnisonpioneermuseum.com/second-confession

Connecticut:

"Annabelle", warrens.net

Delaware:

The Morning News Wilmington, Delaware Mon, August 2, 1948 Page 6

gristfromabbottsmill.net/post/andrews-lake-tragedies-and-a-gruesome-legend

npgallery.nps.gov/NRHP/GetAsset/NRHP/73000493_text

Florida:

newspapers.com/article/the-palatka-daily-news-ghost-story-1888/168405198/

The Palatka Daily News Palatka, Florida • Sun, Jan 29, 1888Page 1

The Palatka Daily News., August 19, 1884, Image 4

Georgia:

home.heinonline.org/blog/2023/08/heinous-histories-the-murder-of-mary-phagan/

The Atlanta Constitution Atlanta, Georgia Wed, April 30, 1913 Page 2

The Atlanta Constitution Atlanta, Georgia Sun, July 20, 1913 Page 7

Did Leo Frank kill Mary Phagan? 106 years later, we might finally find out for sure. - Atlanta Magazine. atlantamagazine.com/news-culture-articles/did-leo-frank-kill-mary-phagan-106-years-later-we-might-finally-find-out-for-sure/

Hawaii:

Honolulu Star-Bulletin Honolulu, Hawaii September 27, 1975 Page 11

Idaho:

The Idaho Statesman Boise, Idaho Sun, October 4, 1959 Page 4

Illinois:

Illinois' first female serial killer, Elizabeth reed, was hung in 1845. (2018, October 19). drloihjournal.blogspot.com/2018/10/the-hanging-of-elizabeth-betsey-reed-in-1845-illinois-first-female-serial-killer.html

genealogytrails.com/ill/crawford/news_elizabethreed.html

Indiana:

Indiana University. Research Center for the Language Sciences., Hoosier Folklore Society. Indiana folklore. [Bloomington: Indiana University Research Center for the Language Sciences, etc.].

Iowa:

Quackenbush, Jannette. (n.d.). *Big Book of American Ghost Stories*. 978-1940087689.

findagrave.com/memorial/9484402/arthur_boyd_moore desmoinesregister.com/picture-

gallery/life/2013/12/06/photos-inside-the-villisca-ax-murder-house/3898221/

docublogger.typepad.com/villiscamystery/history/ murderhouse.com/hauntings/.

Kansas:

Lawrence Weekly World Lawrence, Kansas December 2, 1897 Page 7

Lawrence Weekly World (Lawrence, Kansas) · Thu, September 16, 1897

https://eudorakshistory.com/items-of-interest-1

Kentucky:

kentuckybigfoot.com/counties/jefferson.htm

"Pope Lick Monster: The Dark History Behind this Louisville Legend" [Cryptid Atlas]

"Death by Monster or Machine?" [Hangar 1 Publishing]

Louisiana:

Saxon, L. (1969). Gumbo ya-ya: A Collection of Louisiana Folk Tales Riverside Lore

Quackenbush, J. (2021). *Ghost stories and folk tales of New Orleans.*

Maine:

whav.net/2016/10/23/haverhills-cursed-son-jonathan-buck/

Maryland:

unchartedlancaster.com/2024/01/11/the-legend-of-cecil-countys-pig-woman/

Massachusetts:

Berkshire Sampler Pittsfield, Massachusetts October 30, 1977 Page 6

Howes, Marc. Ghosts. Retrieved from hoosactunnel.net

Michigan:

Weekly Expositor Brockway Centre, Michigan December 11, 1884 Page 2

Grand Rapids Morning Telegram Grand Rapids, Mich Jan 3, 1885 Page 1

Minnesota: britannica.com/topic/wendigo

historyboots.wordpress.com/tag/wendigo/ Wendigo

Mississippi:

msfolklore.wordpress.com/2024/07/04/devil-worshipper-road/

Missouri:

Haden, W. D. (1965). *The headless cobbler of Smallett cave: The origin and growth of a Douglas County, Missouri, legend.*

ozarksalive.com/stories/headlesscobblersmallettcave

ksmu.org/local-history/2018-12-21/locals-say-the-legendary-headless-cobbler-was-a-union-sympathizer-in-hiding

Nebraska:

-history.nebraska.gov/wp-content/uploads/2018/05/doc_publications_NH2012Lynching.pdf

-The Oakdale Sentinel Oakdale, Nebraska · Friday, August 30, 1907

-Fremont Daily Herald Fremont, Nebraska September 12, 1907 Page 1

-Omaha World-Herald Omaha, Nebraska · Thursday, May 16, 1907

-The Omaha Daily News Omaha, Nebraska Aug 27, 1907 Page 1

-nebraskahauntedhouses.com/real-haunt/ghost-bridge-logan-creek.html

Nevada:

rgj.com/story/life/2014/09/08/julia-bulette-murdered/15309309/

New Jersery:

today.com/popculture/tv/the-watcher-real-letters read rcna51754

thecut.com/article/the-haunting-of-657-boulevard-in-westfield-new-jersey.html

time.com/6221960/the-watcher-true-story-netflix/

Mystery – The Watcher – Amateur Connoisseur. amateurconnoisseur.com/2022/03/07/mystery-the-watcher/

Terror Tues Dear New Owner: Mysterious Package Co. mysteriouspackage.com/blogs/curators-file/terror-tuesday-dear-new-owner

New York:

Press and Sun-Bulletin Binghamton, New York Oct 24, 2018 Page A5

North Carolina:

Warren, Joshua P. (n.d.). Brown Mountain Lights Morganton, NC

How to find Wiseman's view of the Linville Gorge wilderness. (2022, May 27). nctripping.com/wisemans-view-linville-gorge-wilderness/

Linville Falls Lodge & Cottages 8890 NC-183, Linville Falls, NC 28647. (n.d.). A 2-minute walk from Linville Falls, this rustic seasonal lodge off Highway 221, and just a short drive to Wiseman's Overlook.

North Dakota:

The Ward County Independent Minot, North Dak Nov 10, 1921 Page 1

Oregon:

The Oregonian Fri, October 28, 2016 ·Page 54

Albany Democrat-Herald Albany, Oregon Thu, August 11, 1949 Page 1

Pennsylvania:

The Gettysburg Times November 12, 1926 - Page 1

The Evening Sun Hanover, Pennsylvania October 23, 1990 - Page 47

Standard-Sentinel Hazleton, Pennsylvania September 04, 1893 - Page 3

Rhode Island:

masshist.org/beehiveblog/2018/03/book-review-the-palatine-wreck-the-legend-of-the-new-england-ghost-ship/

South Carolina:

onlypawleys.com/press-release/these-3-pawleys-island-ghost-stories-may-send-a-chill-up-your-spine/

South Dakota:

Lead Daily Call Lead, South Dakota Mon, Nov 8, 1926 Page 1

Rapid City Journal Rapid City, South Dakota March 16, 1986

Tennessee:

-Jasper Mellinger B. Mar 1837 Ohio D. 1901: Smoky mountain ancestral quest. (n.d.). Retrieved from https://www.smokykin.com/tng/getperson.php?personID=I2922&tree=Smokykin

-Mountain Man Caught in Bear Trap, Dies of Starvation;Dying Boy's Tale Leads to Finding of Skeleton Years Later. (1923, December 22). Knoxville News [Knoxville]

Texas:

tshaonline.org/handbook/entries/big-thicket-light

Utah:

The Wasatch Wave Heber, Utah Wed, April 17, 1996 Page 20

History Blazer article on Jean Baptiste

The Ogden Standard-Examiner Ogden, Utah Sun, March 14, 1971

Vermont:

montpelierbridge.org/2015/10/the-true-story-behind-the-legend-of-annas-ghost/

timesargus.com/news/local/ghost-of-anna-still-haunts-vcfa/article_4dcf023c-3002-5a55-9545-f65f5b9bdcdd.html

Virginia:

nps.gov/cuga/learn/nature/

upload/cave-handout2.pdf

nps.gov/archive/cuga/cudjo.htm.

Washington:

seattleterrors.com/top-10-most-haunted-places-in-washington/

West Virginia:

Quackenbush, Jannette Monsters, Cryptids and Mysterious Wild Beasts.

Wisconsin:

dangerousroads.org/north-america/usa/11974-bloody-bride-bridge-is-one-of-the-most-

haunted-places-in-wisconsin.html.

Wyoming:

cowboystatedaily.com/2022/10/22/wyoming-ghosts-runaway-train-haunting-horse-among-30-years-of-spooky-tales-on-frightseeing-tour/

rypn.org/forums/viewtopic.php?f=1&t=35080&p=196770

www.ingramcontent.com/pod-product-compliance
Lightning Source LLC
Chambersburg PA
CBHW070022260626

47159CB00005B/1926